Peng

AT THE SIGN OF THE

DOG
and
ROCKET

With her last term of school finally over, Lilian has been
looking forward to helping Dad in the pub while Mum
is away with the kids. But now that Dad has slipped a
disc and is under doctor's orders not to move for two
weeks, how is she going to manage? She certainly has
no time to put up with the irritatingly condescending
manner of Tom, the temporary bar help she has to train.

As tempers fray, so the problems mount: they forget to
collect the steak and kidney pies; the dog gets in the way
once too often; Mum phones and is suspicious when she
can't speak to Dad; an Australian tourist arrives wanting
dinner and a bed for the night; and then a customer turns
nasty. Peopled with unusual characters, like Grievous
Hammond and his brothers, this exuberant and hilarious
novel is at the same time a telling portrayal of a develop-
ing relationship and the changes it brings about.

Jan Mark is one of the most highly acclaimed writers for
young people today, and has twice won the Carnegie
medal – for *Thunder and Lightnings* and *Handles*. She
was born in London and grew up in Kent. After studying
at Canterbury College of Art she taught art in Gravesend.
She now lives in Oxford.

+ *Plus* ▸

Other books by Jan Mark

AQUARIUS
DIVIDE AND RULE
DREAM HOUSE
THE ENNEAD
FEET AND OTHER STORIES
MAN IN MOTION

for younger readers:

THE DEAD LETTER BOX
HAIRS IN THE PALM OF THE HAND
HANDLES
NOTHING TO BE AFRAID OF
THUNDER AND LIGHTNINGS
TROUBLE HALF-WAY
UNDER THE AUTUMN GARDEN

JAN MARK

AT THE SIGN OF THE
DOG
and
ROCKET

PENGUIN BOOKS

PENGUIN BOOKS

Published by the Penguin Group
Penguin Books Ltd, 27 Wrights Lane, London W8 5TZ, England
Penguin Books USA Inc., 375 Hudson Street, New York, New York 10014, USA
Penguin Books Australia Ltd, Ringwood, Victoria, Australia
Penguin Books Canada Ltd, 10 Alcorn Avenue, Toronto, Ontario, Canada M4V 3B2
Penguin Books (NZ) Ltd, 182–190 Wairau Road, Auckland 10, New Zealand

Penguin Books Ltd, Registered Offices: Harmondsworth, Middlesex, England

First published by Longman Group UK Limited 1985
This edition published by Viking Kestrel 1987
Published in Penguin Books 1988
1 3 5 7 9 10 8 6 4 2

Printed in England by Clays Ltd, St Ives plc
Typeset in Linotron Melior

Chapter One

Officially school was supposed to end as usual at three forty-five, but by lunch-time it had wound down so far that there was no chance of setting it going again. Lilian Goodwin and Gina Murphy, who were both leaving, stayed in the canteen until the very last moment with their feet up on chairs — they did not quite dare to put them up on the table — and lounged about until Mrs Clarke, the head dinner lady, told them to go away.

'Where are we supposed to be next?' Gina said, as they ambled along the corridor for the last time, past coathooks and discarded sweaty plimsolls.

'Search me. I can't even remember what day it is.' Lilian flicked dead flies from the dusty concrete window-sills. 'This place is a filthy hole.'

'Friday. Hey, last Friday at school, ever. Let's celebrate. What shall we do?'

'Blow it up? Doing nothing's a celebration,' Lilian said. She led a busy life at home and she could not expect another day as idle as this for a long while. 'We ought to go and say goodbye to everyone — staff, I mean.'

'What, Foskett and Anderson and Wiley — and Old Rope?'

'Well, we shan't see any of them again, shall we, unless we go looking for them.'

'I wouldn't go looking for Old Rope with a flame-thrower,' Gina said. 'Funny, isn't it, how we quite liked him in the Lower School?'

'He didn't teach us then. We quite liked old Collins too, when he first came.'

'He never taught me at all.'

'He tried to teach me.'

'Well, he won in the end.'

'Like hell he did,' Lilian said.

Old Rope, Mr Roper, the Deputy Head, was genuinely old, almost due to retire. Old Collins, however, was only a student. When he first appeared at the William Farrar-Langton Comprehensive, Lilian had thought that he looked too young and frail to be on the wrong side of the teacher's desk and had set out to be kind to him, but he had made it quite clear that he wanted no favours, and although young he was not at all frail. After that they had crossed swords several times a week and at the end of his teaching practice Lilian, with one or two others, had given him a bilious send-off, secure in the knowledge that they were not likely to meet again. She was not best pleased, and could hardly believe it, when she saw him coming towards them down the corridor.

'See what the wind blew in?' Gina nudged her.

'Oh hell, what does he want? You'd think he'd have

gone back where he came from by now. The college must have broken up ages ago.'

'Where *did* he come from?'

'I dunno. Up North somewhere, I suppose. Eeee, but he don't half talk funny,' Lilian said, loudly enough for him to hear. She knew it was childish, but it was a good imitation.

'Hey up,' Mr Collins said, cautiously, as they drew level.

'Hey up and hey off,' Lilian said. He could not do anything about it now. Gina rarely bothered to say anything; dumb insolence was her speciality. She simply stared at Mr Collins, revolving upon her own axis and watching him walk away. They could tell that he knew she was staring by the way he accelerated.

'Am Ah going too *fast*?' Lilian said, just as he used to say it in class. She was sure it was the way that he spoke that had finally set her against him; after all, he looked pleasant enough. Several of them had quite fancied him at first, before he opened his mouth.

No one in the history of the school had ever fancied Old Rope, although there was reputed to be a Mrs Old Rope somewhere in the background. As Lilian knew very well, you could get quite high on making life wretched for some teachers. It was impossible to get high anywhere near Old Rope; he could bring on an all-time low just by walking into a classroom, but she and Gina knocked on his door anyway and went in to say goodbye. He was so surprised that he actually smiled at them through his moustache, like a crypt opening to reveal coffins, as Gina remarked afterwards.

From Old Rope they moved on to the Headmaster himself, and then ran into Mr Foskett, on his way out to blow the whistle at the end of lunch break.

'Well, my lovelies, I'll be sorry not to see you two again,' said Mr Foskett, heavily gallant. He patted Lilian on the arm and pinched Gina's cheek.

'If that'd been my bum,' Gina said, as he strolled away, 'I'd have bit him in the leg.'

It hardly seemed worth going back for afternoon registration, so they made a final tour of the field. Round behind the hawthorn hedge they stumbled over four outstretched legs and discovered Peter Sills and Shaun Webb, smoking cigars in the shade.

'Thought you'd be along,' Shaun said. 'Saw you coming.'

'Aren't you going to First Period?'

'It'll be over by the time we get there,' Peter said, reasonably. He and Gina walked on together. Lilian stretched out in the warm hollow that Peter had left in the long grass beside Shaun.

'When do you leave?' she asked.

Shaun blew a smoke ring. 'Same time as you — quarter to four.'

'No, for France, I meant.'

'Oh, I don't know. Tomorrow lunch-time, I think. We'll get the Dover train. The ferry sails at four.'

'Where will you go first?'

'Paris after Calais. Then Rouen . . . Lyons . . . Perpignan . . . over the border . . .'

'You've got a rotten accent. Old Rope would go mad if he could hear you.'

'He can go as mad as he likes now,' Shaun remarked. He was going to university in September, to read languages.

'He smiled when me and Gina went to say goodbye.'

'You went and said goodbye to Old Rope?'

'And Foskett. He's really pathetic, Shaun, old Foskett is. Really really pathetic. I swear he thinks he's sexy.'

'But harmless.'

'Oh, he's that all right. Hey, guess who else is sloping around.'

'The nit nurse?'

'No, Coathanger Collins. I never thought he'd want to come here again. I wonder what he wanted.'

'Oh, I ran into him too,' Shaun said. 'He came to return some apparatus he borrowed from Mrs Wiley. He's OK. I don't know why you got your knife into him.'

'He was so . . . I don't know, Shaun. So rude . . . condescending. Like we were all idiots and only he knew the meaning of life, the universe and everything. The way he used to look down his nose . . .'

'He could hardly help that,' Shaun said, 'given the length of it.'

'And his accent.'

'He couldn't help that, either.'

9

Lilian sat up. Full of happy thoughts that there would be no more rude teachers and condescending students, she had forgotten what was coming. 'Oh, Shaun, I *am* going to miss you. You will write, won't you?'

'Of course I will.'

'Soon as you get to Paris.'

'Yes, yes. A postcard, if not a letter.'

'It'll be awful,' Lilian said. 'You in France, Gina in Ireland and Pete in Belgium.'

'And you in the pub.'

'That's right. All summer.'

'Well,' he said, 'I can think of worse places to be all summer than in a pub.'

The pub was called the Top of the World and it was at the bottom of a hill. Lilian had been cycling up and down that hill for years, to and from school, but last Friday she had crawled up it and coasted down it for the last time.

It was Sunday 24 July, the last quiet Sunday they could expect for a couple of months, and for the next two weeks every day was likely to be busier than usual, for upstairs Mum was packing for the first holiday away from the pub that Lilian could remember in years. Lilian was in the Public Bar, bottling up, and hearing overhead the thump of footsteps, drawers thudding shut, cupboard doors banging and the squeals of James and Emma. The Top of the World was an old building and any noise made anywhere in it could be heard somewhere else. When she was younger Lilian had lain in bed in her room at the back of the house and had been able to hear everything that went on in the bars at the front; she could identify who was being served, and with what, knew how many pints the Hammond brothers had got through, the moment that Major and Mrs Heathcote arrived and even recognized the clicks as Dad switched the lights on and off to call Time.

Lilian had never heard of a pub where anyone actually called 'Time, gentlemen, please,' and at the Three Compasses, across the common, they rang a ship's bell which was periodically hijacked by the students from the agricultural college. The students seldom bothered to come as far as the Top of the World and when they did it was usually the quiet ones, in twos and threes. Knowing what they could do at the Compasses, where they went in teams, Lilian was not sorry. She was not, in any case, overfond of students.

The feet started to come downstairs and the glasses above the bar rang in their racks.

'Don't you come in here,' Lilian said, under her breath, recognizing the footsteps. There was a double flat crash as they hit the tiles in the passage behind the door and then cantered into the Saloon. James and Emma were never allowed near the bars during opening hours so they took every advantage of the times in between. Lilian could hear them hurling themselves at the easy chairs that she had just arranged after hoovering. Privately she thought that her brother and sister got away with far too much, and *anything* that they got away with meant extra work for someone, but Mum was afraid that they felt the pub took up too much of her time and that they were missing something.

'All they're missing is a good clip round the ear,' Lilian muttered. She had grown up before the days when Mum and Dad had felt guilty about running a pub and neglecting the children. She had never felt neglected. She loved the pub. The first game that she could remember playing was at the end of the unkempt garden with an old shelf propped on two bricks; a bar for her teddy bear who had leaned on it, looking convincingly drunk, through all one summer.

Mum was coming down now, slowly, with the suit-cases. It would never occur to James and Emma to give a hand. At the same time the back door in the kitchen opened and Dad came in from the car-park. Mum staggered into the kitchen and Dad came through to the Public.

'When are you leaving?' Lilian asked. He was driving Mum and the kids into Ashford to catch the London train. 'If you don't go soon you'll miss it.'

He looked up at the clock. 'Twenty past, if we're lucky. If we're not we *will* miss it. Len'll be in just before twelve to help open up and I should be back by one. No problem.'

'Unless the train's late. It is Sunday.'

'Well, you shouldn't be too busy. Len'll hold the fort till I get back.'

He went out. Lilian primed the till, put in the float and filled the water jugs, the pitcher for the Public Bar and the black dolphin that gurgled when you poured from it, which she took into the Saloon through the archway that led to Saloon from Public, behind the bar.

James and Emma had cantered out again, leaving all the chairs out of place, and were slamming up and down the quarry tiles in the passage. Lilian went out to see what was going on. The passage led past the foot of the stairs into the kitchen and was private, but beyond the stairs it turned left, where the pay phone stood, and became a right-of-way between the Saloon Bar and the Gents. It was Lilian's least favourite place in the whole building, an intrusion of public into private. She remembered that when she was little she used to lurk in the kitchen doorway and wait until the coast was clear before running along the passage and up the stairs to bed, not because she was afraid of meeting the customers on their way to the Gents, but because she resented their being on her side of the bar. Nowadays there was no need to run; she could cross the passage in three strides and she rarely went to bed before closing time anyway. James and Emma simply did not care. They cavorted in the passage, inviting shunts with customers, and always made a fuss about going to bed, however busy Mum might be in the bar. Lilian was heartily glad to think that they would be out of her hair for a fortnight.

At the moment they were playing hopscotch,

cheerfully spoiling the tiles, that she had recently mopped, with a stick of chalk pinched from the shelf by the dartboard in the Public. Lilian stood and watched them, hands curling into fists, longing to wallop them both. She couldn't remember Mum or Dad ever laying into either of them, however badly they behaved. Not that she'd been strictly brought up herself, but she could not imagine that she would have been allowed to get away with the kind of things that James and Emma did, like wrecking a tidy bar or spoiling a clean floor.

She left them to it – only another ten minutes, she told herself – and went into the kitchen from where Dad was already ferrying luggage to the car, through the garden and the side gate that led to the customers' car-park, and Mum swept past her to collect the children from the passage. Lilian thought, no one ever stands still here. We're always passing each other. If we had tail-lights and someone took one of those long-exposure photographs, there'd be thin red lines all over the place.

'You're going to be all right, aren't you?' Mum said, hurrying back again with a child in either hand. 'It's not going to be too much for you?'

'Of course it's not.' Lilian was impatient. For weeks Mum had been wasting her little spare time in drawing up timetables, as if Lilian and Dad and Len hadn't known to the day, to the hour, to the minute, when things were supposed to happen: the brewers' deliveries, the cigarette-machine man's visit, the shopping, the ordering, the bottling up, the crating of empties, cashing up and banking. She followed Mum out to the car. In passing the sink, Mum had whipped up a J-cloth and was wiping chalk from the children as they went.

Lilian watched them pile into the car, flustering, flapping, arguing, with a descant of last-minute instructions from Mum. Then all four doors slammed and the car rolled away round the corner, across the forecourt and out on to the Dover road in a storm of summer dust.

She stood on the garden step for a moment, watching the dust settle. The air was very still over the hot tarmac; to her right the downs hung heavily under the dark blue sky and ahead the traffic droned along the road to the coast. There were still three quarters of an hour before Len came down from Uppings, the private nursing home where he worked as a gardener, to help open the pub. Lilian turned back into the garden and closed the gate.

It seemed even hotter in the garden. Already, at the end of July, the grass was parched from the baked soil, the few flowers looked stringy and the lumps of chalk on what had once been the rockery glared whitely in the sunshine. No one ever had time to do anything to the garden except run a mower over it occasionally, and if Lilian wanted flowers for the Saloon she went out on to the common. It had lain untouched for years. Over in the corner she could see the bricks that had once supported her teddy bear's bar, undisturbed since Ted ordered his last pint and reeled away into retirement under the stairs. She was glad to turn from this desert into the cool kitchen. She took out the mop from the cupboard and went through to the passage to swab away the hopscotch scrawl on the tiles. From the shady bars came the scent of old smoke and stale beer that some people hated, and that Lilian thought was the most civilized smell in the world.

In the Public the heavy wall clock clunked above the bar, five minutes fast to be on the safe side when calling Time. She put away the mop, washed her hands and went to the fridge to fetch the Scotch eggs, cold meat and salad for the buffet cabinet at the end of the bar in the Saloon. From the garden the Yak came in, his toe-nails clicking on the tiles, sighing and sloshing loudly in his water bowl. He was a large dog, called the Yak because he looked like a yak. He'd never had any other name and he spent most of his time loafing about on the forecourt, trying to cause accidents. When he grew bored with this he went into the Public and embarrassed the customers by looking ill-treated. He liked a drop of stout, but he was not supposed to have it. This didn't mean that he did not get it. Lilian instantly lowered the flap of the bar and closed the little gate beneath it so that he could not surge through later in a hairy whirlwind, as he did at every opportunity. He was very fast on his feet when he scented Guinness in the air.

It was always like this just before opening time on

Sundays. During the week there was an air of urgency that began at seven o'clock when they all got up and did not subside until they closed at two-thirty, but Sunday trade was always slow to come in. In half an hour she would unlock the door of the Public, draw the bolts on the French windows in the Saloon and retire behind the bar to whip away the glass cloth that covered the pumps. Len would do the same in the Public, and they would be ready to go.

Chapter Two

At five to twelve Len came down from Uppings and at twelve exactly, they opened. At ten past Mr Piggot walked over from the alms houses across the road, complaining bitterly, as he always did in summer, about the traffic on the A20.

'One of these days,' Mr Piggot said to Len, 'they'll bring me in here on a shovel.'

Lilian had no customers yet. She propped herself against the bar and looked at the colour supplement, thinking that although a full house was what they needed, and would get, this was the pleasantest way to spend Sunday. The best thing about it now was the absence of James and Emma and she looked forward to the next fortnight with just her and Dad, Len in the evenings and Mrs Allott who came to clean but did not serve: all adults. Then she remembered that Dad had advertised for someone to help in the bar, starting next week. The someone was due to be interviewed tomorrow and suddenly the future looked a little clouded. They had summer help every year; strangers who sometimes lived in and sometimes not, but still intruded, had to be taught, helped, supervised, often by Lilian herself, often resenting a schoolgirl's showing them the ropes. This time, however, she was no longer a schoolgirl, and with luck might have some influence over Dad's choice.

Cars were beginning to draw up on the forecourt. The Yak clicked out to make a nuisance of himself and Lilian put the magazine away under the bar. There would be no chance to look at it again until closing time.

It was after one before Dad returned. He came in through the kitchen, rubbing his back and limping slightly. 'Did you see what your mum put in those suitcases?' he said, 'because it felt like bricks. Pull us a pint, love.'

'I should go and sit down,' Lilian said. 'Put your feet up in the sitting-room and I'll bring it through to you. There's not much going on in here.'

She followed him into the sitting-room carrying the pint of bitter. 'Did they get off all right?'

'After a fashion. The train was late, of course, no buffet, crammed with people, kids all over the place. It looked like hell's delight, but I told her to go in First and pay the difference. She's not used to trains.'

'Nor are you.'

'At least I don't go looking for the strap to open the window with. She can't have travelled by train since the Coronation. What are we doing about lunch?'

'I made up some rolls with the end of the ham. It didn't look too good in the cabinet – and there's some tomatoes and lettuce.'

'That didn't look too good in the cabinet either, I

suppose. I saw them in the fridge – which reminds me, Lil –' she hated being called Lil '– it's time we got defrosted again. If we don't do it soon we'll need dynamite.'

She nodded. 'There's a sardine frozen into that block under the ice tray. Couldn't we leave it for the help? Mum always does.'

'The what?'

'Whoever we get to help out.'

'Your Mum was saving the oven for that.'

'I thought we might do something to the garden as well.'

'We say that every year. It never gets done.'

'But we ought to have a go at the side,' Lilian said. The side garden, next to the Saloon and leading to the gate of their own private garden, was a patch of lawn where customers could sit at tables, but it opened on to the forecourt and was very exposed.

'You've got plans for the side bit?' Dad asked. 'You'll be taking over before long.' He was not entirely joking. One day she *would* take over.

'We ought to put up a trellis and train something over it. Clematis – something like that that grows fast. Or some of those *Cupressus leylandii*. You can buy them four-feet high and they're really fast growing. They cost a bit more that size, but we'd have a decent hedge in a couple of years.'

'Clematis? *Cupressus leylandii*? What have you been reading?'

'Major Heathcote's catalogue.' Major and Mrs

Heathcote ran a garden centre. 'I was having a chat with him about it the other night.'

'You *will* be taking over,' Dad said, and this time it did not sound as if he was joking at all.

Mum and Dad always rested in the afternoons. Today Dad rested alone and Lilian, resting on Mum's behalf, lounged on the settee in the Saloon with the Sunday paper and a bowl of fruit. Len had gone back to Uppings, so the house was quiet except for the monotonous zip of passing traffic which was hardly disturbing to someone used to it. By now Shaun would be in Paris, but it would be silly to look for a letter tomorrow, or even on Tuesday. Perhaps by the end of the week . . . She stopped dreaming and looked at her watch.

They would have a lively evening, with tired travellers coming home from the coast and breaking the journey back to London. At ten to five she took a cup of tea up to Dad and at five he came down to start preparing for the evening, while Lilian set out a high tea in the sitting-room. When the help came that would be her province, also the manufacture of Scotch eggs for which the pub had a considerable reputation. Lilian was no cook. She heard Dad on the stairs and then there was an outbreak of barking and swearing in the passage. He and the Yak had collided, both heading for the gate under the bar.

Mum rang at nine to say that they had all arrived safely, and once that worry was out of the way the evening passed pleasantly, coast trade in the Saloon and locals in the Public (except for Major and Mrs Heathcote who were definitely Saloon): Mr Piggot, the Hammond brothers, Jack Lovell from the service station, Mac and May Bryce who came for the darts, Ambrose from the shop across the field. There was one coach but it was half empty, and the agricultural college had gone down for the summer vacation at the beginning of the month. When the students did come they could be spotted crossing the common, from far off, coming over the knoll among the pine trees on the horizon with the setting sun behind them, like heavies in a Western.

They closed at ten-thirty, cashed up, carried out the crates, said goodbye to Len and locked the door behind him. Lilian collected the glass cloths, turned out the lights and left Dad scuffling about among the crates by the glow of one lamp burning above the bar, while she went to make a last cup of Ovaltine. Suddenly there was a shout.

He's fallen over the Yak again, she thought, but went to see anyway. The Yak was sprawling on the stairs, innocent and looking it, but Dad was still in the bar on hands and knees.

'Did you bang your head?' Lilian said, alarmed. She could see that he was in pain.

'It's my back,' he said.

She tried to raise him.

'No,' he said. 'Don't, Lil – don't. I can't move.'

'Don't be daft. Come on, Dad.'

'I'm not joking, Lil,' he said. 'I can't.' And he couldn't.

Dr Fellows sketched a nasty little diagram on the back of an aspirin packet to illustrate how discs slip. Lilian thought that it looked like a blanched almond being pinched out of its skin, and said so.

'More or less right,' said Dr Fellows, edging along the passage to the kitchen. Very occasionally he turned up in the Saloon with his wife and they were David and Moira, customers, but now he was a busy GP with a long list of waiting patients. Lilian let him out through the kitchen door and hurried with him to the side gate.

'Now remember,' the doctor said, 'he's going to be a shocking patient. If he stays on his back he could be up again in a fortnight – and if he's careful afterwards. But I know him. He'll be raring to come downstairs the moment he hears my car start, staggering about, trying to lift things.' He was already in the driving seat. 'Then it could be six weeks or more and he'll be worse than ever with June away. You must keep him in bed. Can you get Sally Allott to come in and give a hand?' The key was in the ignition.

'Not more than she does already. She goes to Uppings when she doesn't come to us, and she works at the garage in the afternoons.'

'I don't know how that woman keeps going. What about Mrs Len?'

'She comes over funny. You know that.'

'Oh god, yes; so she does.'

'We're getting someone to come in over the holiday to help out, like always. She's coming this afternoon.'

'Make sure she can lift things, then.' The car began to roll. 'Well, I won't keep you. You've got work to do.'

Haven't I just? Lilian thought, watching the car slew round on to the forecourt. Not twenty-four hours ago she had stood here on the step watching Dad drive Mum and the kids away. Now Mum was in Edinburgh and Dad was flat on his back with boards under the mattress, and they were due to open in twenty minutes.

She had crept down very early that morning to stack the empties, bottle up and prepare food for the buffet. In a few minutes the bus would come by and she would have to run across the road and flag it down to collect the steak and kidney pies sent out by Mrs Cutler from Ashford. Best to go and have a quick word with Dad now and use the bus as an excuse to nip down again fast before he had a chance to start arguing. She ran back through the garden and the kitchen and up the stairs, yelling, 'I heard you! Get back into bed!'

Dad was sitting on the edge of the bed in his room at the side of the house, which looked out over the car-park. 'I heard all that,' he said, nodding at the open window.

'Then you know what Dr Fellows said. Lie down again.'

24

'Don't be damn silly,' Dad said. 'How can I?'

'I've got to go over for the pies,' Lilian said. 'I'll be up again later.'

'You can't open up on your own.'

'I can. There won't be much happening just yet and I've managed so far.'

'There ought to be three of us in the bar by lunch-time.'

'All right, then,' Lilian said, evilly. 'Stand up, then. Just stand up and see what happens.' She looked at her watch. 'I've got two minutes; go on Dad. Stand up.'

He looked at her, shifted slightly and gasped.

'Well?'

He lay down again. 'All right. I'll be good. You're worse than your mother.'

'I'll get the pies,' Lilian said. 'I don't want them going on to Maidstone. Then I'll be up again to make sure you're all right before I open. Will you want to go to the loo?'

'I can manage that, dammit!'

She was half-way downstairs. 'You might have to lean on me getting there.'

She dived under the bar in the Public and out through the door on to the forecourt, already late. She could see the bus breasting the top of the hill beyond Uppings, and made the usual suicidal sprint through the traffic to reach the request stop on the far side of the road before the bus did. They had never missed the pies yet. That was going to be the trouble. Everything at the Top of the World ran according to schedule; it had to. No one was ever late. The business of running the pub had become an art and all the artists were masters. Up till that moment Lilian had thought that she must be very nearly a master too, and now she saw that she was hardly even an apprentice and very soon she would have another apprentice to train alongside her. She put out her hand and the bus shuddered to a halt, the pies were handed out in their string-bound cardboard box and the bus moved on. Lilian went back across the road into the Public, and through to the kitchen where Mrs Allott was making coffee.

'I'll take your dad one up and you can take yours through to the bar. I'll have my twenty minutes and then I'll be doing the bathroom. Just give us a yell if things get bad.'

How bad can they get? Lilian wondered, kneeling by the warming drawer of the stove and packing in pies. We've never had just one person for both bars after eleven before.

There was exactly half an hour after closing time to gobble the stew that Mrs Allott had left, take a plate up to Dad and tidy the bar and herself, before the bar help arrived to be interviewed. Dad was getting difficult again. 'Suppose he won't do? How are you going to get rid of him?'

'Him?'

'Didn't I tell you?'

'No, but it's just as well. He'll be able to lift crates. We've always had a barmaid before.'

'That's only because girls were always the first to apply. This one's a bloke – a student –'

'A student! Not from the Agric?'

'I don't know where he's from. But what are you going to do if he gets stroppy?'

'Whop him with a pool cue,' Lilian said.

'I'm serious. Look, I'd better come down.'

'You better hadn't. If I think he'll do I'll bring him up and show you. If I don't I'll tell him we'll let him know. Lie *down*!'

She ran back downstairs again. She had no idea how the applicant would arrive, but if he were coming by bus he could arrive at any moment. The bus from Ashford was already overdue. She took off her apron, tossed it over the bar in the Saloon and went to kneel on the window-seat overlooking the road and the side garden, to be ready for bus or car or bicycle. She hoped he would be on the bus. That might mean he would have to live in and there would be an extra pair of hands twenty-four hours a day to help in the bar, and in the house, the garden, to help with Dad, to lift . . . to lift . . .

The bus came into sight and halted at the request stop. There had been no one waiting to get on so there must be someone getting off. She stood well back from the French windows and looked out as the bus drew away. There, waiting on the far side of the road to cross over, was Mr Collins. Lilian had not thought of its being that kind of a student. She stood in the middle of the Saloon Bar and said 'No!' out loud, and then 'It can't be *him*,' just as people did in plays so that you would know what they were thinking.

But it was him. He crossed the road, on to the forecourt, and stared about him, first at the door of the Public, then at the French windows, not seeing her there in the shadowy interior. Then he advanced and knocked on the glass of the French window. She opened it and there he stood, looking very much as he had done at school, only now wearing cords and a windcheater instead of a suit.

I'm going to enjoy this, Lilian thought. She said, 'Good afternoon, Mr Collins. Have you come about the job?'

Mr Collins said, 'Oh my godfathers.'

'Come in,' Lilian said. 'How nice to see you.'

Chapter Three

Business associates were invited into the bar and given a drink, but Dad normally interviewed prospective bar staff in the sitting-room. Lilian had intended to do likewise but now she saw who the prospective bar staff was, she decided to conduct the interview here in the Saloon. She could not bring herself to take Mr Collins into the sitting-room where she would be just a girl talking to one of her teachers. It would give him a terribly unfair advantage. Here in the bar the advantage would be all hers and he would be nothing more than another young man in search of a job.

Then she had a second thought. The Saloon was too relaxing with all these easy chairs and the settee and the carpet. He would lounge. She remembered seeing him in the staff room, sitting almost on the back of his neck, with his legs stretched out, sprawling. And he would drawl at her in his irritating Northern accent that flattened anything that came within earshot. Mr Collins, meanwhile, was still standing on the threshold with his jaw slightly dropped. Lilian found that an encouraging sight. She opened the door that led through to the Public. 'Come in here,' she said. 'I'm interviewing in the Public today.'

'You're interviewing?' Mr Collins said, following her. Lilian sat down at the little table near the bar where Mr Piggot always settled. That was a mistake. It was like being at a desk again while he stood over her, staring in amazement at what she had written. He was staring in amazement now, and he was also standing. She found herself saying, 'My mum and dad own the pub but Mum's taken the kids on holiday and Dad put his back out last night, so I'm running it now.' That sounded fine, but it all came out like an excuse for getting to school late, and she only just in time bit her tongue to stop herself from adding, 'Sir'.

Instead she said severely, 'Sit down.'

He sat and began to look reassuringly uncomfortable.

'Now,' Lilian said, 'for starters, what's your name?'

'You know my name,' he said, irritably.

'Not all of it. We always called you . . .' She thought of what they had called him and paused, substituting tactfully, 'Mr Collins.'

He said, 'Thomas. Tom, if you like.'

Lilian began to laugh. 'Tom Collins?'

'What's so funny about that?'

'It's a drink – a cocktail. Tom's gin. Where were you brought up?'

'Not in a pub,' Tom Collins said. Lilian did not care for the way he said it.

'I suppose you think we sit around all day boozing. There isn't time. When Mum and Dad aren't working they're asleep. It won't be so bad for them now that I've left school, though.'

'That can't have been much fun for you,' he said, 'when you were little.'

'There's two littler than me. Mum's taken them up to Gran in Edinburgh. It's the first holiday she's had for years. I'm going away for a week fishing with Dad in the autumn – we're having to take turns and the summer's nicer for the kids, only it's busier, too. That's why we need extra help.'

'That's me?'

'It might be,' Lilian said, tartly, 'if you suit.'

'Do you do all the hiring and firing round here?'

'I do at the moment.' She was afraid that the interview might get out of hand and he would start interviewing her. 'Have you worked in a pub before?'

'I've never worked anywhere before except TP and voluntary work.'

'TP?'

'Teaching practice.'

Oh, that's brilliant, Lilian thought. 'Why start now?'

'I need the money. I haven't got a job, yet. Only twenty-nine of us have, out of fifty.'

'Oh.' She had never thought of teachers having difficulty finding jobs. 'It's hard work.'

'I'm used to that.'

'Not like teaching.'

'I did three years at Manchester University before that.'

31

'Not like that, either. There's a lot of lifting. Long hours. Up early and late to bed.'

'Up early and late to bed sounds familiar.'

'You'll have to help out with everything; cooking, cleaning and that. Washing. I'm not going to do it all and Mrs Allott can't.'

'Do I get behind the bar?'

'I hope so. Len's here in the evenings but if his wife comes over funny he has to go home. Mrs Allott comes most mornings, but she doesn't serve. Then there's the shopping . . . am I going too fast?'

She pronounced it as he did, as he always had done in class, in the way that managed to suggest that everyone was much slower on the uptake than he was. He knew what she was about and blushed slightly. Aha! Lilian thought, gleefully; not so tough; but there wasn't much else to be gleeful about. He didn't look tough at all, but terribly lean. He had been known as Coathanger at school since it was put about that this was what he had instead of shoulders. She had heard somewhere that thin men were often wiry, but she knew only too well what happened to wire coathangers. There were five of them in the guest bed-room upstairs, bowed out of shape like overworked paperclips.

Remembering the guest-room she said, 'And this is an inn. We have to provide accommodation – some-times people want a room. And there's the garden.' It would be nice if somebody could do something about the garden. Watching him across the table she measured him mentally, width of shoulder, depth of chest, circumference of wrist. Would he be able to shift kegs, pick up a crate? He did not look as if he could lift a full pint. Could you get a hernia at that age? What use would he be if the Public got stroppy one night, or, worse still, the Saloon, which was a different kind of stroppiness.

'I don't mind what I do,' he said, 'so long as you pay me.'

'How soon could you start?' She hoped she did not sound too eager.

'Tomorrow, if you like.' Evidently she did sound eager, for he added, 'Or tonight, if you're really pushed.'

'You'd better come up and see Dad about money, then. When you've finished I'll show you round.'

'You're taking me on, then, Miss Goodwin?'

She looked him right between the eyes. 'Yes, Mr Collins.'

She went back down to the Public and listened to the creaks and murmurs overhead which were Dad, trying to be imposing in bed, and Tom Collins, feeling awkward, she hoped, in the wheelbacked chair by the window. After a while she heard footsteps and he began to come downstairs. Lilian stood up from where she was kneeling to tidy the boxes of sweets under the bar and intercepted him at the corner of the passage by the pay phone.

'When do you start?'

'Do you want me tonight?'

'Tomorrow will do. There's a bus back to Ashford in ten minutes. Oh!' She hesitated. 'You *are* going to live in?'

'Oh yes.'

'I'll have your room ready. It's got the hot tank in it and it makes funny noises, but you'll be too tired to care. Now, I'll just show you the bars before the bus –' The private telephone began to ring in the sitting-room. She left him in the passage and ran to lift the receiver. 'Hallo? This is the Dog and Rocket.'

'Hallo, Lilian. It's Len.'

'Oh . . .' She knew what was coming.

'Look, I'm sorry, it's Doreen. She doesn't think she'll be able to cope this evening. Has the new chap turned up? Will you be able to manage?'

Lilian looked out along the passage to where Tom Collins was still standing. '*Can* you make it tonight?' He nodded. She was relieved, but annoyed; already in his debt. 'It's OK, Len. See you tomorrow, with luck. Don't worry. Thanks for ringing.' It was not going to be OK, but at least she would not be left entirely alone. She hung up.

'What did you call it?' Tom Collins asked, when she joined him.

'What?'

'This place. I thought it was the Top of the World.'

'No one calls it that. Look at the sign on the way out and you'll see why.'

She saw him through the Saloon and locked the

French windows behind him. As she turned away she saw him standing on the forecourt, beside the Yak, at the foot of the sign that swung in a frame on a tall white-painted post. It was supposed to show a polar bear, sitting on top of a globe with his nose pointing towards the North Star, but the thing was so strangely painted that the star, with a long beam of light flaring from it, looked like an exploding firework, and the polar bear resembled a white bull-terrier. Lilian couldn't recall when she had last heard a regular refer to her home as the Top of the World. She lived at the sign of the Dog and Rocket.

'Well,' Dad said, reclining flat as Dr Fellows had insisted, 'you get all kinds behind a bar.'

'What did you think of him?'

'Very pleasant. But really, a psychologist . . .'

'A what?'

'He's got a degree in psychology. Now he wants to be a teacher. Would you want a psychologist teaching you?'

Lilian shrugged elaborately. Evidently Tom Collins had not let on to Dad that he had taught her, or tried to. She had supposed that he'd emerged from his three years at Manchester with a degree of some kind, but it had not occurred to her to wonder what it was in. 'He'd better not try psychologizing the customers. I wonder what he'll make of the Hammonds.'

'If he's got any sense he'll just serve them. He'll

have enough trouble trying to understand Grievous. Can you fetch me a drink, love?'

'Do you think you should?'

'I don't see why not, but I didn't mean that kind of drink. Just something to wash down these tablets that David Fellows left.' He pointed to the box of pain-killers on the table by the bed.

'Is it very bad?'

'Bad enough. I'm all right if I don't try to sit up.'

'So you won't be trying to *get* up?'

'I won't. You'll be on your own tonight, you and Len.'

'Len can't come – no – it's all right, stop thrashing about. Mr Collins is going to start tonight.'

'*Mr* Collins? That stick? Can't you call him Tom?'

'I think he's probably quite strong – you know, Dad, wiry.' Here was a problem. She did not intend to go on calling him Mr Collins, but she wondered if she would be able to bring herself to call him Tom.

'Well, if he's got to jump in at the deep end it might as well be tonight. Mondays are usually quiet . . .'

'I bet this one won't be,' Lilian said gloomily. 'We'll get three coaches, the Dover Hell's Angels and the Dagenham Girl Pipers, all at once.'

Tom Collins arrived at five-forty, dodging danger-ously through the traffic with a briefcase and a long, blue nylon holdall.

'What've you got in there – a body?' Lilian asked as she let him in through the French windows. 'You needn't come this way again. You can use the side gate in future, like us.' She took the briefcase so that he could manoeuvre the body bag through the doorway. 'Why this? You're not still studying, are you? You won't get much time for that. Oh, hurry up. We open at six.'

'I brought everything with me. I've been staying with a friend since we came down,' he said. 'You can open when you like, *after* six, can't you?' he added, as she rushed him across the Saloon, towards the stairs.

'Yes, but *I* like to open at six sharp,' Lilian retorted. 'This is your room, next to the bathroom. You can unpack later. Just dump your stuff and come down to the Public and I'll show you the price list. Can you pull a pint?'

'No.'

'Can you work a cash till?'

'Of course I can't.'

'Then come on.'

They clattered downstairs again. Lilian threw off her apron as they went. 'That's the rule,' she said. 'We never wear aprons behind the bar.'

'I never wear an apron at all.'

'You may yet. Wait till you start on the fridge – and the oven. Right, now, along here we've got the bottled ales –'

'I can see that.'

'Cans are on the cooler.'

'And that.'

'This is the best-bitter pump, this is the mild. This is the draught Guinness. Now, these drip trays —'

'Hang on,' he said. 'What happens at six? Do you open the doors and stand back while the whole population of the village charges in?'

'No.' She glared at him. 'I don't suppose anyone'll be in until about half past, except Mr Piggot. He'll be on his way already.'

'And what does Mr Piggot take?'

'A pint of mild and bitter, *always*.'

'Well then, you show me how to pull a pint when Mr Piggot arrives. I'll pick it all up as I go along. Just explain the cash register to me now and give me the price list so I can start learning it off. I'll never remember anything, otherwise.'

Lilian turned to face him so that she could glare properly, this time. 'Dad said you were a psychology student.'

'Graduate. That's right.'

'Isn't that all about how people's minds work?'

'Well, basically,' he said.

'You're not very good at it, then,' Lilian said. He flushed, as he'd done when she mimicked his accent at the interview that afternoon, and said, trying to make a joke of it, 'A lot of it's rats.'

'We aren't rats,' Lilian said. 'We're people — and we aren't at school any more,' she went on cruelly, and this time added 'Sir' on purpose.

At half past six the Hammonds arrived. Tom Collins, who had just pulled Mr Piggot's second pint, after a fashion, saw them lined up on the far side of the road, gaped slightly and said, 'Are they coming here or are they waiting for a bus?'

'Those are the Hammonds. They're coming here. Six brown ales, please, in jugs – the glasses with handles.'

'Mugs. Are they trouble?'

'No they aren't. None of the regulars are trouble. Right, now, if you're mixing draught beer and bottled ale the bottle goes in first. Tilt the glass or it'll foam all over. Same with lager and lime or shandy. Lime and lemon in first.'

'How do you know what they'll want?' The Hammonds had found a gap in the traffic and were on the way over.

'They never drink anything else, just brown and mild.' She pointed to the shelf of Gaffer brown ale. 'This is their row. Now, fill up with mild . . . slowly. That's it. You can serve them, then they'll get to know you.'

'You make them sound like shy wild creatures,' Tom said.

'Rats?' Lilian said, nastily. 'There's someone in the Saloon – get on with it.' She went under the arch into the next bar and left him to it, staring nervously at the door of the Public where the Hammonds were coming in.

There were twelve Hammonds, six of drinking age. Modest and silent, none of them was under six feet two. They were builders, and John, the eldest, employed the other five; as well as two younger brothers. Also present were Brian, called Brain because of the way he spelled his own name. Mervyn, Eric, Arnold and Grievous. Grievous was the least shy and acted as spokesman for the others. Unfortunately he had lost his top front teeth and only those who knew him well could understand what he was saying. Lilian, serving her Saloon Bar customer with dry Martini, listened to Tom enjoying his first encounter with Grievous and his missing teeth. It was a long while before she heard the sound of the till. Evidently Grievous was having as much difficulty understanding Tom.

She looked round the corner and saw the brothers standing in a mute circle at the bar, while Tom hovered uncertainly by the till. When he noticed her watching he approached and muttered, 'Don't they ever sit down?'

Lilian realized that she had never seen a sitting Hammond. 'No, they'll stand there till eleven. They'll want another in about ten minutes, so be ready, and another at quarter past. They slow up after that.'

'At that rate they'll get through the whole shelf by the end of the evening.'

'They will, but remember, other people drink it too. If it looks like running out, fetch in some more. I hate to see an empty shelf.'

'Yes.'

'And when you serve the next lot, wipe the bar first. It looks bad to have slops. There's a cloth by the sink.'

40

'Sink?'

'Under the bar – for washing glasses. You might as well fill it with water now. As soon as you get any empties, rinse them out. Glass cloths are on the rail, the other side. When you get a quiet moment go round and collect the empties off the tables. Then you could nip up and see if Dad needs anything. He doesn't even know you've arrived, yet.'

'It seems to me,' Tom said, 'that it wouldn't matter if he knew or not. I can see who gives the orders round here.'

'Good,' Lilian said. 'You've got another customer. Jack Lovell. Draught Guinness. Pint to start with, then a half. Don't forget to fill the sink – then go up to Dad.'

'And what will the landlady be doing all this while?' Tom asked, retreating to the Public.

'What I do here's my business,' Lilian said. She went into the kitchen and fetched the trays of salad from the fridge. There had been no time to set them out earlier.

'Can you make Scotch eggs?' she asked, as she passed him on the way back. He was lifting down the Hammonds' second go of Gaffer brown, under the quizzical eyes of Grievous and his brethren.

'I'm a dab hand with a deep-fat frier.'

'Fine, I'm . . .' She was about to say 'hopeless', but not caring to admit this weakness, said instead, '. . . too busy.'

'You'll have to show me how, but I'll soon pick it up. I do a lot of the cooking at home.'

'Good. Ale in *first*. We're famous for our Scotch eggs.' He began to smile. 'You haven't filled the sink,' Lilian snapped.

Chapter Four

It was a fortunately peaceful evening. At closing time Lilian locked up and left Tom drying glasses while she ran upstairs to give Dad a progress report.

'How's he doing?'

'Not bad. He had a bit of trouble with Grievous.'

'Who doesn't? Remember that girl we had the year before last; would have it he was making improper suggestions?'

'Grievous never made an improper suggestion in his life. I wish he'd get some false teeth, though.'

'Doesn't hold with them – at least, I think that's what he says. He seems to regard them as a sign of old age. He'd rather muddle through with the gap.'

'We're the ones who have to muddle. How's your back?'

'About the same. Listen, Lil –'

'Don't call me Lil.'

'Sorry. When your mum phones, don't tell her what's happened or she'll chuck the holiday and come belting back.'

'Would Gran keep the kids?'

'Would you?'

It was the first time that Dad had even hinted that he thought James and Emma were getting out of hand.

'I won't tell her. D'you want any Ovaltine?'

'If you're making it.'

'Tom can make it.' She paused at the door. 'He can make Scotch eggs, too.'

'By the time you've finished with him,' Dad said, 'I reckon he'll be able to do anything. Treat him gently, Lil. He's only a kid.'

Oh, Mr Collins, Sir, I wish you could have heard that, Lilian thought, as she went downstairs. Mr Collins, Sir, was folding glass cloths on the rack.

'They go in the bin by the sink in the kitchen,' Lilian said. 'We don't use them twice without washing them. Now take the crates out to the back yard. We'll stack the empties in the morning before we bottle up. Do you drink Ovaltine?'

'Yes please.'

'Then make enough for three and take one up to Dad.'

'What are you going to do?'

'I'm going to cash up. Go on. *Shift*.'

Lilian was up before seven the next morning, and was pleased to hear the Collins alarm clock ringing stridently from behind his door as she came out of the bathroom. It was a long time before he switched it off, though.

Sleeping soundly, Lilian thought. He'd better be well awake when he gets down here. By the time he joined her in the kitchen she had made the coffee, put the towels and glass cloths in the washing-machine and was going through the freezer making a list of ices that needed ordering. As he came along the passage she said hollowly, from the freezer, 'Coffee's on the stove. Do you eat breakfast?'

'Toast,' he said.

'Bread's in the bin, toaster's on the table. When you've done I'll show you how to stack the empties and then we'll bottle up.'

She swept past him and went to open the windows in the bars to stir the fug a little. The mail was lying on the mat in the Public, all manila envelopes and no postcards. Still, it was early days yet. She forgot about Shaun and went into the Saloon to check the bills and revise the list that she had made of all the things Tom could do before opening time. She had put 'oven' at the top of it, but now it looked as if the oven, as usual, would have to wait, along with the fridge. Tom wandered in while she was doing it, toast in one hand, coffee in the other.

'If you drop crumbs,' she said, 'you'll have to clear them up.'

'I thought you said you had a Mrs Allott in to clean.'

'Not every day – not Tuesdays,' Lilian said. She pushed the list along the bar. 'Here you are – forget about the oven – start with the hoovering in here, then sweep out the Public. There's spray polish for the wooden tables and Brasso for the copper tops in here. Put out fresh beer mats then –'

45

'Aren't we going to stack empties and — what was it — bottle up?'

'This is for after the empties. We bottle up when you've hoovered. Do the bar after the tables and wipe down the glass shelves, and don't forget the pies.'

'What do I do with the pies?' He looked at the list. 'It just says "pies" here.'

'You fetch them off the 9.45 bus from Ashford. We have them sent in. If you switch on the warming drawer at 9.30, you can put the first pies in to heat up as soon as they arrive. I'll see to the buffet.'

'That's nice of you,' Tom said. Lilian looked at him sharply.

'If the phone rings, answer it and then fetch me. You won't know what to say.'

'If you thought I was so stupid and lazy,' Tom said, 'why did you take me on?'

'Who said anything about being stupid and lazy?' Lilian said, quickly. She did not look at him but saw his reflection in the mirror behind the liqueur bottles. He looked honestly angry. 'I just haven't got time to explain everything beforehand.'

'You'd have a lot more time if you explained things properly,' he said. 'Then I'd know exactly what I was supposed to be doing. It was just the same at school with those essays. You always got angry if I made you tell me what you'd been trying to say. If you'd worked it out before you wrote it you'd have known, and I wouldn't have had to ask.'

'Don't talk to me about school!' Lilian shouted,

jumping down from her stool at the bar. 'Don't ever mention it again. You're lucky I didn't tell Dad what you were really like.'

'I'm lucky? Suppose I'd told him about you?'

'And let him know what a dead loss you were?'

'I passed my teaching practice.'

'Oh yes.' She jeered. 'And you've got a degree in psychology. Fat good that will be if someone starts a fight. You're supposed to be able to understand people. You can't even understand Grievous Hammond.'

'Who?'

'Grievous. The one who does the ordering.'

'Why d'you call him Grievous?'

'It's his initials. GBH.'

'Grievous Bodily Hammond,' he said as she went out. 'I like that.'

'I don't care whether you like it or not,' Lilian muttered, heading for the passage.

'And I like old Grievous. He offered me a pint.'

She put her head round the door again. 'Didn't you take it?'

'I was a bit rushed then. We had those three blokes in wanting Black and Tan and I didn't know what it was.'

'Never refuse a drink,' Lilian said. 'If you don't want it then take the money and have it later.'

'Suppose I don't want it at all?'

'It's a *sale*. You don't miss a sale.'

47

'I bet *you* don't,' he said as she withdrew once more calling, 'the Hoover's in the cupboard in the kitchen.'

She ran upstairs to the bathroom. As a rule the house came second to the pub where cleaning was concerned, but the rule was relaxed for the bathroom. Mum always insisted that no matter what else was neglected, the bathroom must be cleaned in case they should have a visitor in the guest-room. It needed only twenty-four hours for a build-up of discarded shoes, an overspill of dirty clothes from the laundry basket, the appearance of a tide-mark round the bath, whiskers in the sink and hairs in the soap. Lilian attacked it with a damp cloth, noting, as she did so, the intrusion of a strange razor on the shelf above the basin, and feeling vaguely surprised to think that Tom Collins actually needed to shave. It was the first time that she had thought of him as an adult human being with hair and fingernails that grew.

A man. She said it to herself and then again, aloud. She was treating him as a half-witted child and not even enjoying it; but how else was she to manage? 'Give him an inch and he'll take a yard,' she said to the mirror behind the shelf, and saw her face sharpen and turn shrewish. She did not enjoy that, either.

The Hoover was humming in the Saloon. Tom was pushing it back and forth and consulting his list as he went. She was pleased to see that he had stacked the chairs before he began. Even Mrs Allott did not

48

always do that. She signalled to him to switch off so that he would be able to hear her.

'I'm going across to the shop now,' she said. 'I won't be long. When you've finished in here sweep out the Public and then you can fetch the crates from the cellar. Just look at the shelves and you'll see where everything goes. I've left a list of what we need by the till.'

'Where's the cellar?' Tom said. 'I mean, I suppose it's down under, but how do I get in?'

'We've got two. The real one's so small we can only keep the draught barrels in it. Bottles and kegs and cans are in the bit built on at the side. The door's next to the Gents. I left the key with the list. You can switch on again now.' He glowered.

The Hoover was working its way up to a gusty moan as she went out, skirting the Yak who was lurking in the passage. Tom and the Yak had so far avoided meeting each other head-on although Tom, not knowing the Yak and his lust for Guinness, had allowed him to get through the gate under the bar last night, after which he had staggered about, groaning, until Jack Lovell, a fellow stout-lover, had bought him a half which Tom had pulled, not knowing who it was for.

She added a necessary warning about the Yak's drinking habits to the mental list of things to tell Tom as she went out through the gap in the hedge to the shop across the field to buy salad for the buffet. Ambrose always put aside the best vegetables for the

Dog and Rocket and often came across to eat them at lunch-time with a pint and one of Mrs Cutler's pies or a Scotch egg.

Lilian thought of the pies as she came back again. The bus would be along shortly and she wondered if Tom would remember to go across the road to flag it down, but as she dumped the shopping on the draining board, on the way to remind him, the telephone began to ring in the sitting-room. By the time she had dealt with the caller it was ten to ten and coming out of the sitting-room she ran into Tom, hurrying through the kitchen with her list in his hand.

'Those pies . . .' he said.

'Where are the pies?' Lilian cried simultaneously.

'What time are they due?'

'Due? They're *overdue*. Has the bus gone by?'

'One has. That's what reminded me.'

'Which way?'

'Towards Maidstone.'

'That was *it*!' Lilian stared at him, horrified.

'Well, they're still on it, then,' he said. 'Can we catch them when they come back?'

Lilian forgot Dad, within earshot upstairs, and shouted, 'We've never missed them before. That's the first time!'

'But you didn't put the time of the bus on the list.'

'I did.'

'You did not. It just says "pies", look.'

'But I told you the 9.45. I did. I remember.'

'Yes,' he said, slowly, 'but you told me a lot of other

things too, and I'm supposed to remember them all. You should have written it down. I've done everything else that you asked.'

'I wasn't asking,' Lilian said, 'I was telling you. We've never lost the pies before, not since we started having them sent out. You'd better get on to the bus station at Maidstone and ask them to put them on the next one back. Then you can take Dad a cup of tea. I'm going to open up.'

'Before ten?' he remarked, sourly.

'I've got to see what sort of a mess you've made bottling up,' Lilian said, starting for the bar, but it was immaculate, every bottle and can in place in Saloon and Public, the tables polished, the chairs neatly arranged, beer mats on every table. Then she noticed that the water jugs had not been filled or the clean glass cloths put out under the bar. Tom was just leaving the sitting-room after ringing the bus station. As he went to switch on the kettle she called, 'You didn't fill the jugs or put out the glass cloths.'

'They weren't on the list.'

'You should have *known*.'

As she said it she remembered that she had not listed the clean towels for the lavatories either and had to run to see to that. The Dog and Rocket opened at an unprecedented three minutes past ten.

'We never open late!' Lilian said, as Tom came downstairs from delivering Dad's tea. He put his head into the Public.

'Look,' he said, 'I don't have to work here.'

'I thought you needed the money.'

'I do, but I could earn it somewhere else and I'd sooner do without altogether than stand around listening to you rant – to cover up your own imcompetence,' he added, unwisely.

'You shouldn't stand around, then,' Lilian said, but lowering her voice. *Ranting*? 'I haven't got time to.'

'You would if you had things properly organized.'

'They are properly organized. We aren't usually in this mess.'

'You're *not* in a mess,' Tom said. 'If you'd only calm down you'd see that everything's getting done. At school –'

'I told you not to mention school!' Lilian turned on him in a rage but at that moment the door of the Public opened and Mr Piggot came slowly in, followed by the Yak who had been basking on the forecourt. They leaped apart and stood facing the bar to turn welcoming faces to him. It was a fearful effort.

Mum rang again on Wednesday night, but Lilian was serving and it was Tom who answered the telephone. After a moment he came through to the Saloon.

'I'll take over,' he said. 'It's your mum.'

Lilian hesitated. She'd not yet let Tom loose in the Saloon, where people tended to order more complicated mixed drinks. She dreaded to think what he might do faced with a request for Pimms, with its floating salad.

'Two gin and tonics for this gentleman, a Scotch

and soda and a lager and lime. Lime in first. Don't put the tonic or soda in, just open the bottles.' She ran to the sitting-room.

'Mum?'

'Lilian! Where's your dad? Who answered the phone?'

'That was Mr . . . Tom Collins. He's the student who's helping out.' There she stopped. In the panic of the last couple of days she had not stopped to consider what excuses to make when Mum rang again and wanted to speak to Dad. What could she say? On Monday she'd said that he was busy in the bar, but it wouldn't work twice. She said cautiously, 'He's resting. He's got a bit of a backache.'

'A backache!' Lilian could feel the shock waves all the way from Edinburgh. 'What sort of a backache?'

'Nothing much, but it seemed silly not to rest it. Len and Tom are in the bar with me. Tom's fine.' She was surprised to hear herself say that for she did not think that Tom was at all fine, but lies were the order of the day at the moment.

'Has the doctor been?'

'It's not bad enough for that. But David and Moira were in last night —' another lie '— and he said to take advantage and rest it.'

'Advantage of what?'

'Well, we aren't too busy for three of us to manage. Look, Mum, it's OK. How are the kids?'

'They're all right.' Lilian could hear shrieks in the background. 'I want to speak to your dad.'

'He's asleep.' He was watching athletics on the portable telly. Tom had fixed it so that he could see it without raising his head.

'Can't you wake him up?'

'It does seem a pity. We were ever so busy this morning.'

Mum was beginning to sound suspicious. 'Are you sure everything's all right?' There was a crash in the passage. 'What was that?'

'Someone's fallen over the Yak, I expect.' She expected that it was Tom who had fallen over the Yak while fetching in extra bottles from the top cellar. 'Look, Mum, I'll get Dad to ring you tomorrow.' Somehow or other they would have to get him downstairs. 'OK?'

'All right.' Mum sounded very dubious. 'Don't overdo things. Make sure that new fellow pulls his weight.'

'Yes, Mum. Goodbye.' You should watch me making sure he pulls his weight, Lilian said to herself as she ran into the passage to see what had caused the crash. It was not Tom and the Yak, but Mac the darts player and the Yak. Mac, who had been out to use the pay phone, was staring at the remains of his pint glass scattered across the tiles. Lilian also fell over the Yak, and then Tom, who came out to investigate. He scrambled to his feet, helped Lilian to hers, assisted Mac to pick up the fragments of glass and mopped up the spilled beer. Lilian stood over him.

'Don't you know yet that the Yak shouldn't be out here during hours?'

'He's not on the list,' Tom said, rising. He did not sound very amiable, or look it, standing there with the remains of Mac's glass in his hand.

'I told you what a nuisance he is. He should be outside.'

'If he's such a nuisance it's a pity you don't have him put down. Nuisance! He's a bloody menace on the forecourt, that dog. I've seen him cause two near misses in three days.'

'All the regulars manage to avoid him.'

'These weren't regulars. One chap had kids in the car. For god's sake, keep the stupid animal shut out of the way. It's stoned out of its mind half the time.'

'How dare you tell me how to look after our dog.'

'You *don't* look after it, for Christ's sake. Anyway, I'm not bothered about the dog. I don't care if he's ironed out by a bus. It's people I'm worried about. This place has as many locks as a dungeon. Can't you manage to keep him in?' He strode past her, seized the Yak by the collar that lay somewhere under his hair and dragged him, still sitting, along the tiles, through the kitchen and into the sitting-room. The door slammed and the Yak set up a fearful hooting wail. Lilian had never heard him howl before and ran to comfort him, but Tom barred the way. 'Leave him alone. If I've to keep him out of the bars, this is how I do it. Understood?'

Len looked round the archway. 'If you've both finished, we've got a few customers in here want serving.'

Lilian pushed past Tom. 'Psychologist!' she said, loudly enough for him to hear, as she went by.

Chapter Five

Next morning the Yak looked haggard and glared at Tom from under his melancholy fringe, but he kept out of his way. Lilian arranging the buffet, thought it made a nice change not to be continually tripping over him.

'I can't *show* you how to make Scotch eggs,' she said. 'I can *tell* you.'

'Tell me later.' Tom was crawling backwards downstairs with a tape-measure. 'If your old man can walk as far as the end of the landing, I can get the phone to the top step.' Lilian had already fetched the pliers from the cupboard under the sink. He began to remove the staples from the telephone cable that snaked along the skirting-board, through the Public Bar, across the stairs, along the passage behind the freezer and into the sitting-room. 'We'll have to put them all back neatly. British Telecom doesn't like its equipment mucked about with.' He looked at his watch. 'Pie time. Can you go across today?'

'I know it's pie time,' Lilian said quickly, but she said nothing else. It had been no fun seeing Tom lose his temper last night, out in the passage. It had been great fun at school, when he was just Mr Collins, a mere student with no authority and too stupid to see where he had been going wrong. She went out across the road and stood by the bus-stop, reflecting that she and some of the others had spent much of that last half-term trying to make Mr Collins lose his temper, and that possibly it was not stupidity but genuine niceness that had prevented him from complaining to anyone. In a way it was stupid to be so nice in a school like the William Farrar-Langton, but then they would have been far worse, in a more subtle fashion, if he had reported them. That's what a psychology degree does for you, I suppose, Lilian thought, and she looked up to find that the bus was almost upon her, and she flagged it down, imagining what Tom might say and certainly would think if *she* let the pies travel on to Maidstone.

That evening Dad creaked along the landing and made a phone call to Mum.

'Everything's fine. Everything's fine,' he was saying, into the receiver. He sat stiffly on the upright chair at the very brink of the staircase, with the telephone teetering on the top step while Tom lay up the stairs, holding it in place. 'It's nothing, just a twinge; anyway, it's completely cleared up now. Just needed a rest and I got it. The kids held the fort with Len.'

Kids! Lilian thought, in the Public Bar. That's me and Tom. She'd not minded hearing Tom described as a kid, but it seemed less acceptable applied to her, although she was younger.

She went on into the Saloon with the plate of Scotch eggs that Tom had made that morning after transplanting the telephone. He had produced twelve, but the first four had burned on one side, and only the top halves were saleable. While Lilian was upbraiding Tom for his carelessness, conveniently forgetting that she herself had never made a successful Scotch egg, the Yak had eaten the charred halves which they had intended to have for lunch, and Tom clouted him with the greasy spatula. Now, when they met, the Yak crawled away on his belly, looking as if his back had been broken.

Tom came downstairs with the telephone.

'Everything all right? I'll just help Bob back to bed and then I'll be down.'

Oh, it's Bob now, is it? Lilian thought. Is he going to start calling Mum June when she gets back? She said, 'What are we going to do next time she rings?'

'Call me and I'll get Bob along the landing while you keep talking and walking upstairs. We'd better leave the chair where it is for now.' He vanished.

I'd never have thought of that, Lilian confessed. Major and Mrs Heathcote came in and she put down the plate of eggs to serve them. By the time she had finished chatting about Cupressus leylandii and her plans for the side garden, Tom was down again refuelling the Hammonds and setting up Jack Lovell's second Guinness.

'Where's my drinking companion?' Jack asked.

'Watching telly in the sitting-room,' Tom said.

'And he's staying there. Sorry, Jack, but he really shouldn't be walking around on the forecourt.'

'You're so right; don't apologize,' Jack said. 'I've come nearer to a heart attack watching that dog than I have in twenty years at the garage.'

'He's nearly had me off my bike more'n once,' Mac said. 'You any kind of a darts player, Tom? Join us on this side on your night off.'

'No kind of a darts player,' Tom said. 'Now, if it were mah-jong . . .'

'Fill her up, Tom,' Ambrose said, pushing his glass along the bar, and Tom's hand went unerringly to the shelf of McEwan's. Grievous said something too.

'No chance,' Tom answered, over his shoulder. 'He's got two left hands, that lad.'

When he had given John Hammond his change (Grievous was only the mouthpiece), Lilian beckoned him over. 'What did Grievous say?'

'He wanted to know if I thought Stacpoole would be picked for the Third Test. He won't.'

'How do you know?'

'It's obvious. Like I said, he's got two left hands.'

'No, how do you know what Grievous said?'

'I don't know what you make such a fuss about,' Tom said. 'He's clear enough to me.'

Lilian went back to the Saloon, more impressed than she would admit. No one before had managed to understand Grievous in four days flat, and who would have guessed that in four days flat they would be calling him Tom in the Public and asking him to play darts? Who would have guessed that Jack Lovell also disapproved of the Yak? Perhaps some of the others did as well. Perhaps they really should keep him locked up during drinking hours, even after Tom went away. Perhaps James and Emma should be kept locked up too, when they came home. Perhaps Tom would see to it . . .

'Hey up!' Tom said, from the archway. 'You've got customers.' While she had leaned on the bar, wondering, three people had come in and were waiting hopefully to be served down by the buffet, where they were admiring Tom's Scotch eggs in their nest of parsley. She had not really noticed the parsley before and when Tom came through to use the Bourbon optic she said, 'That never came out of our garden.'

'I had a word with Mr Piggot at lunch-time. He'll keep us in parsley, he says.'

'How did you know he had parsley?' Lilian demanded.

'We were talking about his garden last night.'

'Do you know anything about gardens?'

'No, but I'm learning. If I ever have a spare minute I'll have a go at ours.'

Ours? Lilian thought. We *are* settling in, aren't we? She had always hated it at school when he said 'Hey up', but it sounded all right behind the bar; friendly, but not so heartily friendly as Dad's habitual greeting: 'Hello, Squire.' She went into the sitting-room to fetch Major Heathcote's catalogue which he had loaned her so that she could order the cypresses. The

Yak, draped unhygienically over the settee, looked up feebly and moaned.

'Hey up,' said Lilian, without any sympathy at all, and shut him in again.

On Friday Dr Fellows looked in, at a run, and said that Dad was to stay on his back for another week and then they'd see . . . On Saturday Tom got down on his knees to clean the oven, its first mucking out for a very long time. Lilian, bottling up in the Public, could hear him swearing and scraping, since there were many layers of carbon to remove before the cleaner could take effect.

'Fridge next,' she said, as she went to the kitchen to fetch clean glass cloths, but she smiled as she said it. Tom smiled too, in the oven.

'I'll come back next year and do that. What do you cook in here anyway, swans?'

The telephone rang in the sitting-room, its bell echoed by the barking Yak, already imprisoned for opening time in thirty minutes. A woman's voice said, 'Can I speak to Tom, please?'

'Yes,' Lilian said, surprised. 'Who is it?'

'His mother,' said the voice, and Lilian went to fetch him, faintly startled to think that he had a mother. She had never thought about his family at all — somehow you didn't, with teachers. It was always a shock to see them with husbands and wives and children, pushing trolleys in the supermarket or buying disposable nappies in Boots. Come to think of it, she did not even know where he lived. In the week that he had been at the Dog and Rocket they had never had time for ordinary conversation. Any conversation that they did have was mainly a matter of giving and taking orders. It did not sound very pleasant, put like that.

'That was my mum,' Tom said, returning to the yawning pit that was the oven.

'I know. Where was she calling from?'

'Home. Rotherham – near Sheffield. She's very put out that I've not gone home. I *told* her I'd get a job down here, if I could.'

'Didn't she know you were working here?'

'I never had the chance to ring her. I sent her a postcard, Thursday, and I suppose she got it yesterday. Now she thinks I'm going to the bad.'

'Why, because you're working in a pub?' Lilian was ready to feel insulted.

'Oh yes. She makes it sound like a gin palace with winos on the doorstep. I told her, "Look, Mum, you never made a fuss about me working at the William Farrar-Langton. That was far worse." '

'It must have been,' Lilian said, recalling how much worse she and the others had made it for him. 'I thought I might do some gardening this afternoon,' she said. 'D'you want to help?'

'If I ever get out of this hell-hole alive,' Tom said, with his head in the oven. 'But don't expect me to do any digging. Your soil's like concrete. I'd need a pickaxe to get through it.'

'We've got a pickaxe.'

'I don't care if you've got a pneumatic drill and a JCB. This is the wrong time of year for digging.'

'Actually,' Lilian said, 'I never said anything about digging. I thought I might trim the privet round the side and do a bit of weeding.'

'With a screwdriver? OK, I'll help.'

'You can reach the top of the hedge; I can't.'

'I'd rather cut than weed. All right, I'll trim your hedge for you.'

'Thanks,' Lilian said, and realized that she had never said 'Thanks' to him before and perhaps he did too, for as she walked down the passage, carrying the glass cloths, he called after her, 'Can I have that in writing?'

Tom and his long thin arms coped very well with the top of the privet hedge, so well that he had it down to the height of the gate for the first time in ten years. Indoors the oven was really clean for the first time since it had been installed. Lilian, gouging dandelions out of the Saloon Bar window-box with, as Tom had suggested, a screwdriver, looked forward to the time when he zapped the fridge. Distantly they heard the telephone ringing. Tom had his arms full of long privet clippings and Lilian ran to answer it, leaping over the sulky Yak who was asleep across the gateway.

It was another woman asking for Tom, only a much younger voice than before.

'Who's speaking?' Lilian asked.

'It's Andrea.'

'I'll fetch him,' and Lilian went to do it, feeling unaccountably uneasy that Tom should be getting calls from young women. She went into the Saloon to summon him through the side window, and when she heard Tom cross the kitchen and close the sitting-room door she lingered in the passage, almost unconsciously moving towards and stopping outside the door.

'No,' Tom was saying, 'I can't, really I can't.'

'Not till . . .'

'Not till September . . .'

'There isn't time, really . . .'

'No . . .'

There was a long silence, then a wail. 'Aaaandrea, I *can't*.'

Lilian walked quietly out of the kitchen, back to the side garden, and began to unravel the most overgrown of the marigolds from the border. Clearly Andrea was not getting things all her own way. After a bit Tom came out, fell over the Yak, sat down on his rook's nest of privet clippings and put his head in his hands.

'Oh dear,' he said, 'oh dear.'

'Bad news?' Lilian asked.

'Oh, bloody hell,' said Tom.

Lilian said, 'Was that your sister?'

'Not my sister,' Tom said, unhelpfully.

'Have you had a row?'

'The mother and father of. She wants me to go home for my birthday. So did Mum, but she understands about the job.'

'Doesn't Andrea?' She must be his girlfriend. 'You could have the day off.'

'To get to Rotherham and back?' He recited. 'Ashford to Charing Cross, Circle Line to King's Cross, King's Cross to Sheffield, change at Sheffield . . . there'd be a party at the end of it, too.'

'Two days?' Lilian said. There was no question of his having any time off. They both knew that. 'I don't want you to miss your birthday.'

'I shan't miss it, they will. I'll have it here. I was at home last year, anyway. They can't complain.'

'When is it?'

'The sixth – today week.'

'It's nice having a birthday in the bar. How old will you be?'

'Twenty-two.'

'Twenty-two?'

'Don't look so horrified. There's still a week left of twenty-one.'

On Sunday evening Mum rang again. By this time Lilian and Tom had come to a tactical arrangement. It was Tom who took the call and made frantic signals to Lilian who had rushed to the door of the bar as soon as she heard the bell. She ran out, leaving Len, already warned, to cope, grabbed the telephone and gabbled, 'Hallo, Mum. I just wanted a quick word –

Tom's getting Dad – he's serving – we're ever so busy –'
while Tom raced upstairs to fetch Dad, more or less
as she had said. As soon as she heard the bedroom
door open she tiptoed out of the sitting-room, along
the passage and minced up the stairs, talking all the
way.

'Why are you whispering?' Mum asked. Lilian had
not meant to whisper but whispering seemed to go
with walking on tiptoe.

'I've got a frog in my throat,' Lilian said, and
clapped her hand over the mouthpiece as a tell-tale
burst of laughter from the Public threatened to betray
the exact whereabouts of the telephone, half-way
upstairs. She reached the top just as Tom and Dad
arrived at the chair, and handed up the receiver.

'Hallo, love,' Dad said, loudly cheerful to conceal
his wincing. 'How are you – how are the kids?' Tom
discreetly stepped over Lilian to creep away, trod on
her hand, tried to avoid it, slipped and tobogganed
all the way to the foot of the stairs on his back. Dad
jumped violently and Lilian let go of the telephone
which hung jerking from the receiver. Mum could
be heard demanding, 'Bob! *Bob!* What on earth was
that?'

'The Yak,' Dad said, with great presence of mind.
With less presence of mind he leaned forward to grab
the telephone as Lilian started downstairs after Tom,
who had turned an inelegant somersault at the bottom
and was sprawled in the passage. Dad yelled with

pain as his vertebrae ground together, at which point the Yak joined them, bounding over Tom and wallowing upstairs. Lilian had left the sitting-room door open when she came out with the telephone.

Mum was screaming, 'Bob! What is it? Is it a fight? Are you all right? Bob! Lilian!'

Dad was now holding the telephone but had let go of the receiver which bounced down the stairs behind Lilian to be seized by the Yak, panting loudly, in his teeth.

'Are you OK?' Lilian asked Tom, now vertical again.

'No, but I'll live.'

'Have you got a minute, anyone?' Len asked sarcastically, looking out from the bar and backed by a throng of unserved customers. Tom limped into the Public; Lilian crawled upstairs again with the receiver, wrested from the Yak.

'Are you all right, Dad?' Mum was working up to hysterics. 'It's OK, Mum. That was Tom – he fell over the Yak.'

'But all that crashing and yelling!' Mum cried. 'It sounded like a riot.'

It was a riot, all right, Lilian thought.

'What was that heavy breathing?'

'That was the Yak. He got hold of the receiver.'

'Where's your father?'

'He's helping Tom.' Dad was rubbing his back and signalling to Lilian to give him the receiver. She handed it over, mouthed, 'I'll be back in a minute,' and went down to the Public. Compared to what had been happening on the staircase, it was all very quiet. They had at least twenty customers, with whom Len was dealing single-handed, while in the Saloon, Tom, with a great dark bruise coming on his cheekbone, was explaining to Major Heathcote that he had not been in a fight, while trying to serve five USAF officers with five different drinks. In the corner of the Public sat Jack Lovell and the Yak, supping Guinness. Taken all round, it was unusually lively for a Sunday night; quite the most entertaining Sunday night, in fact, that they had had for a long time.

Chapter Six

Tom had such a black eye next morning that he could not prise it open.

'Is it all worth it? I ask myself,' he said, peering at his injury in the mirror behind the liqueurs which, being tinted, made it look even worse than it was. 'Seriously, Lil, would it be so very awful if your mum found out about Bob and came home? I mean, after last night she must think we're wrecking the joint between us. Wouldn't it be better to tell her the truth? She might not come back after all. If we have another avalanche on the stairs she certainly will.'

'She would come back and yes it would be awful. You can't imagine how awful it would be.' Lilian looked up from the list she was making for the brewers' order. 'You've forgotten about James and Emma.'

'Well, I've not actually met them yet, remember.'

'You will on Saturday — special birthday treat. That'll be fun. Honestly, Tom, you wouldn't believe how bad they are.' She was about to remind him that they ought to get on with the cleaning, for upstairs Mrs Allott was banging about in the guest-room, but before she could, Tom went on with what he had been doing, wiping down the shelves behind the bar. Lilian finished her list and went to telephone the brewers. When she came back he was bottling up in the Public.

'Have you polished the tables?'

'Not yet. Sorry.'

'Nor's Mrs A. I'll do it.' She fetched the cans and cloths from the kitchen and went to attend to the woodwork in the Public Bar first, to keep Tom company.

'It was all right when they were small.'

'Who?'

'James and Emma. Then James started being a pest when he went up into the Juniors, and one of the teachers told Mum that he might feel neglected and then she started worrying. It was old mother Haddaway. She had me in the Juniors too. She never told Mum I felt neglected.'

'Perhaps you didn't.'

'I was never a pest.'

'You made up for that later.'

Lilian rubbed hard at a sticky patch and did not look up. 'Emma didn't even have to be a pest at school. Oh Tom, it's so *annoying*. I mean, Mum was run off her feet before I left school, but as soon as one of those little monsters wanted something she'd drop whatever she was doing and run after them. And they won't get up in the morning, or go to bed when they're told – only they're never really *told* to do anything. And they turn this place into a pigsty. Like, the other day, just before you came, they drew hopscotch all over the tiles after I'd mopped out the passage. And they scrawl on mirrors, and pinch the darts. I caught James on the pool table playing with a gardening cane and a stone, and Mum hardly said anything. I mean, if he'd torn the cloth . . .! And Emma whines all the time. They aren't allowed in the bars during hours so she stands out in the passage and whinges. And Mum comes out. *Always*. She even actually leaves *customers*. It's embarrassing. And then I lose my temper and she lets fly at me. This could be a really brilliant place if it wasn't for those two. Really really good.'

'It seems fairly brilliant to me already,' Tom said, turning from the shelves. 'I hope you ordered some more barley wine. Stocks are getting low.'

'Yes, I did. It's not, Tom. Not like it could be. We ought to be able to do proper food, and have music . . .'

'God forbid.'

'Real music. There's a really good jazz band does pub gigs round here.'

'What I like about this place is that there *isn't* any music. Or fruit machines, or space invaders. Anyway, how would you fit a jazz band in, and all the extra customers? Which band is it?'

'The Hot Dogs — they're from Thanet. We could put them in the barn — across the car-park. I mean, it would need a lot done to it, but it would be worth it. And if only we could get the garden really nice, we could have more tables and do functions in summer –'

'Functions?'

'I hate pubs where the tables are all anyhow and the grass is all bald patches and covered in fag-ends. That's what it'd be like if we did it now. I keep trying to do something about that bit at the side. I've ordered some bushes. Dad doesn't know and he'll probably go spare when he finds out, but the Major gave me a discount. Dad's always saying I'm trying to take over. I'm not – but I will one day.'

He smiled. 'Will you?'

'I don't see why not. Just wait till the kids leave home . . .'

'All right,' he said, 'you've convinced me. We don't want your mum back before time.'

'Oh, it's not just that,' Lilian said. 'It's not really that at all. This is the first time she's been away for ages. She's with her mum – they hardly ever meet. I don't want it all spoiled for her.'

'Blu-tak!' Tom said.

'You what?'

'We'll stick the phone to the top step with Blu-tak. No more avalanches. It'll mean us all using it up there, but it's only for a few more days.'

'So it is.' Lilian had not thought how few. Suddenly she wanted things to go on just as they were.

Tuesday was the day the brewers called. Last week Lilian had supervised the delivery herself, not daring to entrust the job to Tom who had been there not even one day.

'This is what I ordered,' she said, giving him the list. 'You make sure that it's all there, or that they tell you if it isn't. When they've done they get a pint of what they fancy. I've got to go over to the Post Office.'

'Ashford?'

'No. There's one in the village. If the chap about the cigarette-machine comes, he knows what to do.'

'Is he on the fiddle too?'

'I never said anyone was on the fiddle. Just keep your eyes open.'

The village was on the far side of the common. Lilian crossed the road, turned down the track past the alms houses and on to the footpath. It ran downhill a little way, through birch trees, and as soon as she was among them the monotonous sweep of the traffic was cut off as if a window had been closed. Down there among the bracken all she could hear were the bees; even the birds were quiet and the smells of oil and diesel that hung over the A20 were replaced by the damp scent of fern roots, the late-flowering wild honeysuckle and the less attractive but peaceful smell of stagnant water in the ditch.

The low-lying parts of the common were sodden even in summer and the footpath ran over hillocks to avoid them, but Lilian took her private short cut along the shoulder of the great concrete drainage-pipe that ran straight from one side to the other.

She was half-way across before she noticed that she was skipping and stopped, looking round guiltily to see if anyone on the footpath was staring down at her antics, but she was alone in the great hot hollow of the common, with a couple of passing dragonflies. However, she walked on, more sedately, to the end of the pipe and climbed to the ridge where the pine trees stood, still a little surprised to find herself so cheerful. Yesterday's afternoon post had brought a card showing the Citadel at Namur from Pete and this morning a view of green Irish hills from Gina, but nothing, still nothing, from Shaun.

The village lay below her, shaking slightly in the heat, and she ran down the lane towards the council houses, the shops and the Post Office where it seemed that everyone in the village had urgent business. There was a long queue.

By the time she got back to the Dog and Rocket it was after ten-thirty. The brewers had been and gone and Tom, looking almost smug, was standing at the bar in the Public.

'I opened up,' he said. 'I hope you don't mind.'

'All by yourself?'

'That's right. Haven't I done well? Actually, I asked Bob and he said to go ahead. I wondered where you'd got to. I thought you might have got jumped on crossing the common.'

She thought it was nice of him to have wondered,

although he did not seem to have been particularly worried.

'They don't do that sort of thing round here. There's plenty of people to jump on in Ashford. No one's going to bother to come this far to commit an offence. Been busy?'

'Only Mr Piggot – and a couple of people going to the coast – oh yes, and we'll have a guest tonight.'

'A guest?'

Tom looked worried now. 'Isn't that right? I thought you said you had accommodation.'

'Oh, we do, but it's ages since anyone used it. Who is it?'

'A chap from Australia looking for a real English country pub. He'll only be here one night – he's touring. Kent and Canterbury today, Sussex tomorrow, Hampshire and the New Forest on Thursday. He's got a month to do the whole country.'

'Thirty-one days. But there's more than forty counties.'

'Well, some are quite small. He could probably do Bucks. and Berks. in one day, for instance. Nothing much to look at in Bedfordshire – nothing at all to look at in Bedfordshire . . .'

'Where is he?'

'Oh, he's off seeing Kent. I've got his luggage down here behind the bar. I was just waiting for you to get back before I took it up.'

'How much did you charge?'

'Twenty-five pounds with dinner and breakfast.'

'Dinner! You'll have to cook it.'

'Is Len in tonight?'

'Yes.'

'I'll cook it. Real English country-pub dinner. Roast beef —'

'In this weather?'

'He'll be used to hotter than this — he's from Alice Springs. We'll finish up with rhubarb crumble.'

'Ugh. You'd better nip across to Ambrose at lunchtime and get the rhubarb, and see if he's got any decent beef in the freezer.'

'Can't we go somewhere and buy some real meat?'

'I wish I'd known,' Lilian sighed. 'I could have got something in the village. I don't feel like walking back there again. I'll make you a map of the common and you can go.'

'Look, Lil,' Tom said, 'stop me if I'm talking out of turn, but there's a perfectly good car out there in the car-park.'

'I can't drive.'

'I can. Would Bob let me?'

'I should think so. I'll ask him.'

'If he says yes,' Tom said, 'let's go out this afternoon. Let's go to Canterbury too.'

'This is the first time we've both been away from the place since I came,' Tom said, as they drove over the downs. 'What's the betting Bob gets out of bed and crawls downstairs to see what kind of a hash we've been making?'

'He knows we won't have made a hash, but I bet he goes down anyway, and I bet he gets stuck at the bottom of the stairs. Perhaps we shouldn't have come out.'

'If he's daft enough to get up he can put up with being stuck.'

'We mustn't be away too long. He might be in pain.'

'He's all right on his back. He can lie down in the passage,' Tom said unsympathetically. 'There's plenty of room, don't I know it. Come on, Lil, you're worn out; so am I. We needed a break.'

'I'm not all that worn out – I'm used to it, remember. And I actually ran across the common this morning.' She did not quite like to confess that she had been skipping.

'That's got nothing to do with it. You never really let up. Forget about your dad and enjoy yourself. We can have an early tea somewhere and get back in plenty of time to bottle up.'

'We should have done it before we came out.'

'Stop fussing.'

'And we must find a butcher – for the Australian's dinner.'

'What, roast butcher and Yorkshire pudding? We'll find one.'

'I wish you wouldn't steer with your knees. You're supposed to have your hands at ten to two.'

'I know, but all the blood runs out of them.'

'You must have funny hands.'

'I have.' He made them into trembling claws.

'Stop mucking about. This isn't your car.'

'I think the tappets need adjusting. I'll have a look at them when we get back.'

'There won't be time. You're cooking, remember?'

It began to rain as they passed through the village of Thannington Without.

'I've often wondered about that,' Lilian said. 'Without what?'

'Canterbury, I guess – outside the city,' Tom said. 'Like the green hill far away without a city wall. I never understood that when I was a kid. Why should a green hill have a city wall anyway? I thought.'

'So did I. It would rain. What shall we do?'

'Get wet – or lurk in the butcher's all afternoon,' Tom said. 'Don't be soft, Lil. We shan't dissolve and it may stop, anyway. If it doesn't we can go into the cathedral. You could spend a whole day in there – a week, even – and never see everything.'

They walked round Canterbury Cathedral with the Australian's dinner in a plastic bag. It was a splendidly juicy piece of beef and a little pocket of blood collected in one corner of the bag. Tom said that he felt like a murderer who had deposited the torso in a left-luggage office and was looking for somewhere to leave the head. He felt even more like a murderer when Lilian pointed out that there was a hole in the bag and they discovered a suggestive trail of red splashes behind them on the flagstones. They left the cathedral immediately.

79

It was still raining when they came out but there was a teashop in the Buttermarket, beside the gateway, and they went in there.

'My treat,' Tom said. 'Have what you like.'

'I ought to pay for you,' Lilian said. 'I'm your employer.'

'Have you got any money?'

'Not much. Have you?'

'Now's a fine time to ask. I've got enough but I – I'm not quite sure how to put this, Miss Employer, Ma'am; I haven't been paid yet.'

'Not paid!' Lilian was just sitting down but she sprang up again guiltily. 'Oh, how awful – I'll tell Dad – oh, Tom, you should have said.'

'Calm down – *sit* down. I wasn't complaining. I've only been with you just over a week – but I am running a bit short.'

'And I let you pay for the beef!'

'That was nearly a week's wages too,' Tom said. 'I couldn't believe it when he weighed it out. It's years since I bought any meat.'

'What've you been living on, then?'

'Oh, they fed us at college. The cheapest thing was baked potato with cheese filling. I lived on that, mainly.'

'I thought potatoes were meant to be fattening,' Lilian said.

'I suppose they are, but I didn't often finish mine. The spuds were always cold and the filling . . .' Tom glanced unhappily at a passing plate of oozing cream pastries '. . . the filling looked as if it had been eaten already.'

Chapter Seven

They returned to the Dog and Rocket at five-thirty.

'That was nice,' Lilian said, as Tom parked the car. 'I enjoyed that. Thanks, Tom.'

This time he did not ask for it in writing. 'So did I. Now, a quick coffee and then bottle up or a quick coffee *while* we bottle up?' They walked through the garden gate and across the lawn.

'It'd better be while,' Lilian said. 'You make it. I'll nip up and ask Dad about your money. We can take it out of the till, I expect.'

'I thought he was supposed to be laid out at the foot of the stairs.'

'Oh god, I'd forgotten all about that.' She ran to unlock the back door.

Dad was not at the foot of the stairs. Lilian ran up, skipped over the stuck-down telephone and turned along the landing. The bedroom door was open.

'Dad? Dad!'

He was propped up on pillows, reading a magazine.

'Dad, have you been up?'

'Only to the bathroom. How was Canterbury?'

'You've been downstairs, haven't you?'

'No I haven't. Did you have a nice time?'

'You have. You've been down to see what we've been up to.'

'I don't need to. I can hear what you're up to — through the floor.'

'You'll have a relapse.'

'I HAVE NOT BEEN DOWNSTAIRS! Stop nagging, Lil, you're worse than June when you get going. And I wish you'd stop pitching into Tom.'

'I don't pitch into him.'

'Yes you do, something rotten. You didn't let on that you'd met before, did you. Nor did he.'

'How do you know?'

'Through the floor. Well, I hope you've settled your differences. I'm surprised he didn't walk out, the way you went on at him, Lil.'

'And don't call me Lil.'

'He calls you Lil — and gets away with it. Come on, did you enjoy yourselves?'

'Yes, it was nice,' Lilian said, 'but I can't hang about. We've got to bottle up and Tom's got that Australian to cook for tonight. He's just making coffee. D'you want a cup? It'll be roast beef for dinner — for the Australian.'

'We don't do dinners.'

'Tom does.'

She called down to the kitchen for the extra coffee and went along to the guest-room to make sure that all was ready for the Australian's return. Tom had been up to prepare it during a slack period that morning, but she was uncertain about his housekeeping

83

standards, unnecessarily, it seemed. The bed was neatly made up, he had borrowed a lamp and an ash-tray from the Saloon for the bedside table, the rug from Tom's own room lay by the bed and on the chest of drawers were a runner and a small vase of flowers; the inevitable marigolds out of the side garden. She ran downstairs.

'Tom! Did you do all that in the guest-room?'

'I suppose you thought I'd just leave him a heap of straw. No, it was the fairies. I put out bread and milk for them.'

'It looks lovely. Is that Dad's coffee? I'll take it up and get some money and pay you for the beef.'

'Fairies'll do anything for bread and milk. And a drop of gin. God, Lil, they're dreadful when they get on the booze. Lying around in heaps . . .'

'Shut up, Tom.' Lilian leaned on the bar and giggled.

Tom stared at her. 'Do you know, that's the first time I've ever seen you laugh.'

'I used to laugh at school.'

'Not proper laughing. Not nice.' He looked serious. Lilian felt it.

'I must have been really horrible. And last week, too. Really really awful.'

'You were a five-star ratbag,' he agreed cheerfully. 'All better now, though, isn't it?'

She nodded.

'Good-oh, as Mr Ollerenshaw would say.'

'*Who?*'

'Mr Ollerenshaw, our Australian. Which reminds me, he'll be back at six-thirty if he hasn't got lost. Take that coffee up to your Dad and we'll bottle up. Then I'll start on the dinner.'

Mr Ollerenshaw, Stan after half an hour, said good-oh several times during the evening, most of them while he was having dinner. Lilian laid the sitting-room table with Mum's best linen and cutlery and acted as waitress while Tom and Len served in the bars.

'That was a beaut meal,' said Stan, after she had brought his coffee. 'Why don't you stay and have one with me, if you've got time?'

Lilian fetched another cup and joined him at the table. It was very quiet in the sitting-room, in the fading light from the small window with just one red-shaded lamp glowing on the sideboard.

'Do you do all the cooking round here?' Stan asked.

'I didn't cook it,' Lilian said.

'Don't tell me it was your young man.'

'Tom? Yes it was. He's not my young man,' Lilian said, 'he's bar staff.'

'And kitchen staff too, by the look of it. He's a find. I don't know that he's the type I'd expect to find behind a bar – or you, come to that.'

'You get all types. Anyway, I live here,' Lilian said. 'It's my home. I don't suppose Tom had time to tell you, but Mum's on holiday and Dad's laid up with a bad back, so we're running the place on our own. He only came last week, but I don't know how I'd have managed without him. He's just here for the holiday.'

'More coffee? I'd hang on to him,' Stan advised.

'I can't. He's a student – *was* a student. He's looking for a job as a teacher. No, I won't have any more, thanks. I ought to get on. Will you stay here or would you like to sit in the Saloon?'

'I'll sit in the Public if it's all the same to you,' Stan said. 'Your Tom tells me there's a hot darts player due in at eight.'

'Mac Bryce. Buy him a Worthington and he'll play all night.'

She went to fetch down Dad's plate and transfer the Yak to the sitting-room from her own room, where he had been shut in while Stan was eating his dinner.

'Hey up!' Lilian said to the Yak and the Yak, perhaps recognizing the quotation, bared his teeth.

By Wednesday lunch-time the rain had swept inland and reached the Dog and Rocket. Ragged clouds hid the crest of the downs and the roar of the traffic turned to a liquid swishing. It was so dark in the Public by closing time that they had had to switch on the lights.

'It should be a quiet evening,' Lilian said, 'if it goes on like this. It's a nuisance. I was going to do some more gardening.'

'I should lie down,' Tom suggested. 'You said your mum always does in the afternoons.'

'I don't get so tired as she does. Maybe we could do the fridge?'

'I thought I might go into Ashford to spend some of my ill-gotten gains,' Tom said, 'but it's early closing.'

'It may not be in Maidstone. You could take the car.'

'No . . . it'll be early closing there too, I bet. Anyway, my god, Maidstone in the rain. And Ashford in the rain. Rotherham can't compete, it's too lively. No, we'll do the fridge. It's hell having money and not being able to spend it.'

Tom had been paid at last and Stan had departed earlier, leaving a massive tip on the bedside table. Tom had wanted to share it but Lilian said no, he had done all the work, he should have all the credit.

'Credit's right,' Tom said. 'Out of the red at last. I owe my mum a tenner. I'd better mail it. D'you mind if I ring her this evening?'

'Ring her now, if you like,' Lilian said, locking the door behind Mr Piggot as he plodded away slowly in the rain, across the forecourt.

'It'll be cheaper this evening. It's a long way.'

'You can phone Andrea too, if you want.'

'I suppose I should,' Tom said. 'When was it she rang?'

'Saturday. Do you call each other regularly?'

'Not very, but it's my turn.'

'Have you been going with her long?'

'Going with her? What a horrible expression. I've known her a couple of years.'

'Are you going to get married?'

'I don't know.'

'Does she want to?'

'I don't – look, what the hell's it got to do with you?' Tom snapped, and went quickly down the passage to the kitchen, leaving Lilian to move into the Saloon and lock the French windows there. She stood by them looking miserably at the wet forecourt where the sign was swinging in the wind. They had been on the edge of a row, the first for days. She had not meant to upset him by talking about Andrea. Then she realized that possibly he was not upset, simply annoyed by her curiosity, and she felt more dejected than ever.

After lunch, the cold remains of Stan's roast beef and rhubarb crumble, they switched off the fridge and attacked the gleaming iceberg that had once been the freezer compartment, but they did not enjoy it.

It took until five o'clock to clear the fridge and liberate the sardine, the butter, the tomato, four radishes and a stuffed olive that were trapped in the iceberg. What little talking there was done, was done by Lilian, Tom answering only in grunts or monosyllables. She could not tell if this was because he was occupied with the ice or because he was still angry with her for asking questions about Andrea. When she went back and played the conversation through again it really did sound very like cross-questioning. But I was only trying to take an interest, she told herself. I suppose they're splitting up and he doesn't want to admit it. She wondered how she would feel if he kept asking her questions about Shaun Webb.

Which reminded her — it was twelve days and still no word from Shaun. As she stood by the stove, waiting for the kettle to boil to defrost the next layer, she reviewed the situation. Tom did not know about her and Shaun (for he would never have noticed at school) but if he had known, for instance, that Shaun had not been in touch since he went to France, she would have hated to have him asking questions about them. He must feel the same about Andrea. After all, last time he had spoken to Andrea, they had very nearly been having a row. Perhaps after she had left off eavesdropping they really had had a row; he had been pretty fed up when he came out again.

She thought of Shaun. Shaun, it seemed, had not thought of her for twelve days. The post from France couldn't be *that* bad. Then she realized that she had not thought of Shaun for nearly as long, not really *thought* about him, since the moment when she had heard Dad shout from the bar, the night Mum went away; not, in fact, since Tom came.

She wanted very much to apologize, but she was afraid to invite a snub by introducing the subject. She was glad when tea-time came round and she had an excuse to go up to Dad with a tray. When she came down again the kitchen was empty. The fridge, defrosted, wiped and replenished, was humming in an efficient, self-contained way that she had forgotten, it was so long since she had heard it functioning properly, and the distant clash and clink of cans and bottles told her that Tom was bottling up, rather

crossly, in the Saloon. She went out by the back door
to pick mint for the Pimms and as she came in again
she saw Tom crossing the kitchen to the sitting-room
with the Yak, to shut him away for the evening. The
Yak now walked at Tom's heels when commanded,
surly and sullen, but obedient. Why did we put up
with the hairy great fool for so long? she thought, and
closed the door behind her. At the same moment Tom
closed the sitting-room door and, without seeing her,
hurried along the passage and upstairs. His footsteps
halted at the top; he must be going to telephone. She
could hear him dialling, then, as she approached the
foot of the stairs, he said, ' Hallo Mum.'

Not Andrea.

Good.

But he must have called Andrea later for he did not
come downstairs until nearly half past six, and then
he appeared with a long and furious face, glanced
quickly into the Saloon to see if she were there and
took his place in the Public ready to set up for the
Hammonds.

When Len and a thirsty coach party arrived at
seven, they still had not spoken.

'Had another row?' Len asked, tactfully, when he
came through to the Saloon Bar for pickled eggs. 'I
thought you'd signed a truce.'

'Not really a row – but I think he had one over the
phone with his girl and he doesn't want to talk about
it.' Lilian did not look at him.

'Ah, well. Heard from your fellow yet?'

'No.'

'You didn't have a row with *him*, did you?' Len liked Shaun.

'I expect the post's delayed from France.'

'Very likely,' Len said. He retired to the Public and Lilian, leaning on the bar in the empty Saloon, heard cheerful conversation drifting through the archway; Jack Lovell and Len, Mac and May and Ambrose at the dartboard, toothless Grievous and Tom. There was nothing to stop her from going to the archway and joining in, but she felt too downcast to move; then suddenly Tom was through it himself, clutching at her arm and pointing at the French windows.

'Bloody hell, Lil, look what's about to blow in.'

She looked. A red MG was drawn up on the fore-court and beside it, just locking the door, was Mr Foskett.

'Does he often come in here?' Tom asked. 'You might have said.'

'He never did before — well, not while I was around.'

'He's got a lady with him. Is that Mrs Foskett, I wonder?'

'There isn't a Mrs Foskett.'

'There are probably two or three Mrs Fosketts — oh god, look, he's coming in here. I wish you joy of him.'

'Oh no, no . . . come back, Tom. You serve him.'

'Serve him? You're joking.' Tom was already back-ing through the archway.

'But . . .' The French window was opening. Lilian mouthed at Tom. 'Go on. It'll be easier for you.'

'It won't. He hates my guts. Passions ran high in that staff room.'

Lilian had not thought of passions even trickling in the staff room, but she saw that Tom was looking really alarmed. She shrugged and turned back to the bar. After all, Mr Foskett was just another customer in here; he was no longer her teacher and nothing he might say could upset her; not that he ever had upset her. They had all rather despised him at school; middle-aged, overbearing, stickily chivalrous, never knowing when to stop, he was a nuisance, but a harmless nuisance, unlike Old Rope with his iron eye and forked tongue.

Mr Foskett was closing the door and peeling off his driving gloves. He had not seen her yet – he was talking to his lady. Lilian stared at the lady. She was just about what you would expect to see attached to Mr Foskett. He was wearing cavalry twill trousers, brown boots, cavalry twill cap and a sheepskin car coat. She was removing a silky evening jacket to reveal a little black dress, far too little, Lilian thought. She was quite a big lady; much too big for Mr Foskett.

He slapped his hands on the bar. 'Campari and soda with mucho ice and a double Scotch, on the rocks, *if* you please, my love.'

He's even worse out of school than he was in, Lilian thought. Why did we ever crab about poor old Tom being condescending. She said, 'Good evening, Mr Foskett.'

'Good grief, it's the gorgeous Lilian, looking more ravishing than ever. Claire, this is one of my star pupils.'

Claire, who had a hairstyle like a boiled chrysanthemum, nodded her overblown head in Lilian's direction and smiled at the mirror behind the liqueurs.

'Don't tell me you work in this – place?' Mr Foskett said, leaning his sheepskin elbows on the bar and sending the ice bowl skidding against the gurgling dolphin which belched hollowly. Lilian could have sworn that he had been about to call it 'this dump'.

'I live here,' she said.

'Oh, Lily, my love,' cried Mr Foskett, 'and you with your mathematical mind! You can do better than this for yourself, surely: live-in help with Sundays off?'

'I mean,' Lilian said, passing him the Campari, 'it's my home, I run it with my mum and dad.' Out of the corner of her eye she saw Tom, the real live-in help, lurking cravenly in the Public. Poor Tom hadn't had any days off yet.

'But, my dear girl,' Mr Foskett went on, grabbing at his Scotch and flicking her a ten-pound note as if it were a bus ticket, 'what about your career?'

'This is my career,' Lilian said.

'Can't we sit down, Joe?' Claire said, ignoring Lilian. 'This isn't the easiest place to talk. The others'll be here soon.'

Bleeding cheek, Lilian thought, as Mr Foskett actually bowed to his lady and handed her towards the settee, meanwhile leering at Lilian over his fleecy shoulder. Lilian turned away and began to polish glasses with a fresh dry cloth. On the far side of the archway Tom was inquiring, with exaggerated eyebrows, if it were yet safe to come out of hiding. Lilian smiled at him and thought quite kindly of Mr Foskett. Thanks to Mr Foskett they were friends again . . . well, at least talking to each other.

Chapter Eight

At the top of the stairs the telephone rang and Lilian ran to answer it, glad of an excuse to get out of the bar.

'If he wants another, you can serve him,' she said to Tom, who was hurrying from the far end of the Public.

'No, no, I'll answer the phone,' Tom said. 'You stick to Foskett.'

'Stay!' Lilian said. 'Send Len if you can't face him.' She bounded upstairs.

It was Mrs Len. 'Oh, Lilian, dear, are you busy?'

Lilian felt a drop in temperature. She knew what was coming.

'Not especially,' she said, and it was true, but it was not likely to remain true for very long. Wednesday was often a busy night and the Public was already fairly full.

'I don't think I'm going to be able to get through on my own,' Mrs Len was saying. Lilian found herself nodding understandingly. No one was really sure, not even Len, what it was that Mrs Len could not get through, but she knew that she would have to send him home.

'Don't worry,' she said. 'I'll tell him.' She replaced the receiver and began to back down the stairs. Dad came out of the bathroom and hobbled along the landing. He saw her face descending from sight before she had time to adjust it.

'Trouble?' he asked.

'No, Dad,' she said at once, 'just a message for Tom.'

'Trouble for Tom?'

'Not much,' she said and went on down, thinking that it might well be trouble for Tom if he were landed with Mr Foskett after Len went. There was no question of telling Dad the truth or he'd be on his way down too, to help out. His back was already showing signs of recovery. With luck and caution they would have him up and about by the time Mum came back. No way was she going to risk a relapse now.

'That was Doreen,' she said to Len who was in the Saloon, having just served Mr Foskett with his second double Scotch. And the silly fool's driving, she thought. I wonder if Len knows? I thought teachers were supposed to be hard up.

Len looked worried. 'Can't she cope?'

'No. It's OK Len. We can.'

'Two of you? On a Wednesday?'

'Tom's got the hang of everything now. We'll be all right.'

'I hate doing this,' he said, but he was already reaching for his raincoat that hung on the back of the bar door. He turned to pat her on the shoulder. 'You're doing a great job, Lilian. I don't know what your dad would have done without you. Watch out for the fellow in the sheepskin.'

'Don't tell me,' Lilian said. 'He's my maths teacher.'

'*That*? *Him*? A teacher? I don't know what the world's coming to. He looks like a bookie's runner.'

Len lifted the bar flap and went out through the Public.

'Where's he off to?' Tom asked, coming in from the top cellar with a crate of Worthington. 'Don't say Foskett's put the frighteners on him too?'

'No. Doreen's come over funny again.'

'Have I met Doreen? Would I know how funny she can be?'

'No, you haven't — no one has, except Mum and Mrs Allott. She has nerves.'

'Don't give me that. You're talking to a psychologist, remember.'

'Well, that's what everyone calls it.'

'Out of her tree,' Tom said unkindly, while arranging the Worthingtons on their shelf. 'And we're stuck with bloody Foskett and his bint.'

'Tom!'

'Well . . .' he growled, sullenly, 'look at her.' He nodded through the archway. 'Fanlight Fanny's not in it.'

There was a sudden eruption of noise from the Saloon. They both looked through the archway, Tom very cautiously, and saw that Mr Foskett and his lady had been joined by a number of friends. Two were on the settee with the lady while several more were drawing up easy chairs into a circle. Major and Mrs Heathcote, who had come in while Lilian was answering the telephone, looked on with raised eyebrows as Mr Foskett stood in the middle, loudly taking orders for an unattractive assortment of drinks.

Lilian looked away just in time to see Mac signalling from the end of the bar and went to serve him, basely leaving Tom with no option but to go into the Saloon and deal with Mr Foskett. She felt guilty. But he's older than me, she consoled herself. He's bigger. He can handle it.

She served Mac and May and watched the archway. Mr Foskett came to the bar. Tom, stooping slightly, put his hands on it. He was much taller than Mr Foskett, but he seemed to shrink as Mr Foskett focused on his belt buckle and then began to look up slowly.

'Good evening, Joe,' said Tom.

'Good god almighty, what are you doing here?' said Mr Foskett. He turned to one of the friends. 'They told me this was a good place for a night out. No one said it was an annexe of the William Farrar-Langton. One of our leavers served me just now and here's the last student teacher. I wonder if they've got the Head out back, washing up. Decided not to teach after all, then, Collins?'

'Still waiting for a job,' Tom said. His outstretched fingers were curling up.

'That's not entirely unexpected, though, is it?' said Mr Foskett.

'What can I get you?' said Tom.

'Doing all right here, are you? Who took you on — little Goodwin's old man? And what does little Goodwin think of that? I didn't think you were ever her favourite member of staff.'

Oh my god, thought Lilian. What's he going to come out with next?

'They're good kids, all that crowd, but they did go a bit over the top with you, didn't they? I suppose you realize your supervisor was in the know?'

'Really?' Tom seized his chance to turn the conversation and laid hold of the glasses in Mr Foskett's hands. 'Same again, was it?'

'Not so fast.' Mr Foskett drew back the glasses and said, rapidly, 'A pint of best bitter, if you've got such a thing as a best bitter, a gin and Slim-line, a whisky and ginger ale, a lager and lime, a dry Martini, two Pimms and a double Scotch and a Campari and soda. Got that?'

Tom nodded. Lilian would have gone to help him out but she could not leave the Public with several strangers ready for refills, and she feared to draw further comment from Mr Foskett. Instead she got on with the serving and kept an eye on the Saloon, where Tom was dealing competently with Mr Foskett's order.

'Will you take them with you?' he asked, as Mr Foskett turned from the bar.

'Bring them over on a tray,' Mr Foskett said, without looking round.

Silently Lilian passed him the largest of their tin trays and raised her eyebrows in sympathy. Tom mouthed a quite disgusting comment and went back to arranging greenery on the Pimms. Then he stood the whole lot on the tray, stooped under the bar and carried the order to Mr Foskett's party. Mr Foskett cast his eye over it.

'You've forgotten the dry Martini,' he said. 'This is a bit of a comedown, isn't it? I thought you were the one with the high-powered ideas – headmaster by the time you were thirty, wasn't it?'

'You must be thinking of someone else,' Tom said. He went back to the bar for the dry Martini. 'I only want to teach.'

'There are too many psychologists in this profession already,' said Mr Foskett, when he returned. Lilian noticed that whenever Mr Foskett spoke, Fanlight Fanny and the rest of the friends fell silent, so his remarks carried clearly into the Public, but as soon as he finished they all brayed with laughter which only encouraged him to say something more and worse.

He really has got his knife into Tom, Lilian thought. I wonder if he'd be like this if I hadn't left and he knew he was going to be teaching me again next term. She was very tempted to go into the Saloon as moral support, but just then six lads piled out of a landrover on the forecourt and came charging into the Public, so she had her hands full. They were in a loud good mood, but even above their racket she could hear Mr Foskett.

'Of course, all the girls were after him, and he lapped it up – didn't you, Collins? I said to him, "You're making a rod for your back," but he wouldn't listen. "Just make sure you keep your hands to yourself," I said. "You could be in deep water there. Jailbait." '

How could anyone dislike Tom so much? Lilian wondered, forgetting that not long ago she too had disliked Tom quite as much and had been very nearly as unpleasant.

'What about your bit of fourth-year skirt, eh, Collins?'

Just let him mention *me*, thought Lilian, and her hands clenched round the pump handles.

'If you want any help, you two, just say the word,' Grievous informed her kindly, through his gap, and she nodded gratefully.

Tom came to the archway, and he was shaking. All he said however, was, 'Isn't that three double Scotches he's had? And he came in that souped-up sauce boat. We shouldn't let him have any more, surely?'

'No we shouldn't,' Lilian agreed, afraid to sympathize and glad to talk shop. 'He was half cut when he arrived.'

'I don't know what'll happen if he orders again and I say no. How do you say no?'

Lilian hesitated. 'I've never had to say no. I leave that to Dad or Len.'

'Well, we can't bring Bob down just to throw Foskett out . . .'

'Do you think we'll have to throw him out? Could you?'

'Him and the other eight? Dear god.'

'Perhaps he won't ask for another.'

'Hey! Barman!' Mr Foskett was leaning on the bar and peering through the archway. 'Another lager and lime, at the double.' Tom turned to answer Mr Foskett's insulting summons. Lilian served the Hammonds and Mr Piggot, made sure that everyone had a drink and then ran out to the lavatory, the first chance she'd had since opening time. When she came back, Tom was in the Public, rushing round to collect empties, and Mr Foskett was swimming towards the bar in the Saloon. He thumped on it.

'Where's your swain, then? Chickened out?'

'If you mean Tom,' Lilian said, as civilly as she could, 'He's busy in the other bar.'

'You want to watch him, my love,' Mr Foskett said. 'We had a name for him in the staff room.'

And we had a name for you, Lilian thought. She smiled pleasantly.

'He's got a girl in Rotherhithe, you know.'

'Rotherham, Mr Foskett.'

'Right.' Seeing that he was making no headway in that direction, Mr Foskett turned his attention to more urgent matters. 'We'll have two more Pimms, a Campari, two double Scotches —'

This is it, Lilian thought. She said, 'I really don't think you should have any more, Mr Foskett.'

'What?'

'You're driving. I don't think you should have any more to drink.'

'Did you hear that?' Mr Foskett turned and bawled to his companions. They all jumped. They had certainly heard *him*.

'Have a tonic or a fruit juice —'

'This sanctimonious little cow who was playing footy at the back of my maths class with the school buffoon not three weeks ago, is now telling me what I should be drinking.'

'I can't sell you any more,' Lilian said. She too was beginning to shake.

Mr Foskett became overly polite. One of his friends looked over his shoulder and he said, 'Perhaps you would not object to serving this gentleman?'

'Not at all,' Lilian said, 'But even so, I can't let you have any more alcoholic drink.'

'Perhaps you could come to some arrangement about the driving,' said a voice at her ear. Tom had come through the archway. 'And please don't make any more offensive remarks about Miss Goodwin.'

Lilian wished he had not said that. It sounded unbearably pompous. Mr Foskett evidently thought so too, for he turned to his friends and bellowed. 'Oh, hark at that! Alderman Collins addressing the Licensed Victuallers Association. Eeeh, lad, keep at it. Tha's doing champion.'

'Do shut up, Joe,' Tom said, instantly dropping the Alderman Collins act. 'I'm only trying to be polite. I can't keep it up much longer.'

'Who are you calling Joe?' Mr Foskett demanded. 'Foskett to you, you self-satisfied little creep.'

The little creep, head and shoulders taller, sighed aloud. 'Stop being silly. You can't make us serve you, and if you don't give over arguing I'll call the police before you get out on the road and cause an accident. Please, Joe.'

'Foskett to you, I said.' The rest of the friends were mobilizing.

'All right, Foskett; out.'

'What did you say?'

Tom ducked under the bar and straightened up on the far side. He addressed himself to Mr Foskett's nearest companion. 'Would you be kind enough to take your friend home? He's becoming a nuisance.'

Mr Foskett aimed a swipe at Tom which connected somewhere, but the recoil knocked him backwards and his other arm scythed across the bar top, sending glasses, bottles, ice bowl and the gurgling dolphin shattering down among the crates on the far side. Lilian leaped back as a sharp fountain of splinters sprayed about her knees, and dived under the bar to join Tom who had fallen against the wall and now had a fat lip to balance his black eye. The friends stood in an uneasy but threatening semi-circle behind Mr Foskett who was rocking on his feet. Lilian stared up at them, feeling sick with fear — nothing like this had ever happened before — and drew closer to Tom, but they were no longer alone. Major Heathcote was striding towards them, followed by Mrs Heathcote with her umbrella drawn, and at the sound of the crash the door from the Public had opened. In came John, Brain, Mervyn, Eric, Arnold and Grievous Hammond, Jack Lovell armed with a pool cue and Mac with his darts. Last of all came Mr Piggot, walking-stick to the fore. The regulars had mobilized too.

Both sides stood looking at each other in silence, then the friends began to shift and sidle, and taking Mr Foskett with them, moved towards the French windows. There was a brief angry revving of engines outside, and the episode was over.

Tom, blotting his mouth on his sleeve, looked sideways at Lilian and muttered, 'Call Time, love. It's near enough, anyway. Then go up and explain things to your Dad. I can't.'

Lilian crawled shakily under the bar and flicked the light switches, then headed for the stairs. Behind her, the customers of the Dog and Rocket went into action. Jack locked up, the Hammonds moved round collecting glasses and emptying ashtrays, Mac and May came behind the bar and began to wash up. Mrs Heathcote fetched the first-aid kit from the Public and set about Tom's damaged lip. Even Mr Piggot was wiping up slops.

Half-way upstairs, Lilian heard the bedroom door open. Dad was on his way to see what the row had been about, although given the acoustics of the Dog and Rocket he must have had a fair idea. At the same moment the telephone began to ring, but even so she had to sit down for a moment, she was trembling so violently. It was not only shock. 'Call Time, love', he had said. *Love*.

But he was only being friendly, of course.

Chapter Nine

Len had Thursdays off from Uppings. He was so remorseful about having abandoned them the previous evening, especially in view of what had happened after he left, that he gave up his morning to help out. Lilian had to go to the bank and caught the bus into Ashford. She climbed to the top deck and sat at the back, from where, looking out of the rear window as the bus ground up the hill, she saw Tom come out of the Public and hurry across the road to collect the pies from the Maidstone-bound bus that was just passing hers. He was too far away for his injuries to show, but she knew that close-to he looked as if he had run head-on into a turbine. What on earth was Mum going to say on Saturday?

Lilian was going to buy him a birthday present. She had sat upstairs to enjoy the view but she forgot about that as she engaged with the latest problem. She had no idea of what to get for him and she realized, the more she thought about it, that she knew so little about him that she could not even guess at what he might like. She was determined that after last night it ought to be something special, but what? He didn't seem to care much about clothes, he never had time to read and if he liked music he'd not had a chance to listen to any. She had never seen him doing anything athletic, even at school. He might be a judo black belt, for all she knew, although she doubted it – they'd have been scraping Mr Foskett off the wall if he had been.

What did you give to men? She had made a mental list of all the kinds of presents that Dad liked; mainly useless tools and gimmicks for the bar; nothing that Tom would care for. What about Shaun? She'd not known Shaun long enough to have given him any kind of present, birthday or Christmas. Thinking of Shaun she remembered that he still had not written. She did not care very much, either, and went back to thinking about Tom and his birthday present. Didn't smoke, didn't drink much . . . driving-gloves . . . sunglasses? A book on psychology?

The rain had cleared overnight. Ashford was hot, moist and crowded, not as Canterbury had been, with sightseers, but with irritable shoppers. Lilian went to the bank and queued, to the butcher's, and queued, to the greengrocer's, the Co-op and the ironmonger's; everywhere a queue. She missed both of the buses that she had hoped to catch and still she had not seen anything that would do for Tom. She thought of letting him have the money instead, he could probably do with it, but it seemed a graceless thing to do and she did want to give him a proper present.

She passed a sports shop. Doesn't fish, doesn't run, doesn't row, play cricket . . . ah. She'd heard him talk about cricket with Grievous but he never mentioned it otherwise. Darts . . . but he didn't play darts, either. She distinctly recalled Mac inviting him to join a game and he had declined. 'Now, if it were mah-jong,' he had said.

Lilian had heard of mah-jong before but she knew very little about it. She pushed open the door of the shop realizing, as she went in, that she hardly knew what to ask for. 'Do you sell – er – things for mah-jong?' she asked the assistant. He stared at her.

'Things?'

'Well . . .' she felt herself blushing, 'whatever it is you play it with. Rackets and that . . .'

He nearly fell over laughing. 'You don't play mah-jong with rackets. You buy it in sets, like chess. I'm afraid we don't sell it here.'

Lilian laughed too, with a vision of a mah-jong court with thirty-two squares. 'Who would?'

'A jeweller might – it's a very fancy game – all little tiles. Or a gift shop.'

None of the jewellers stocked mah-jong sets but at last, after missing a third bus, she ran one to earth in a second-hand shop behind the High Street. By now picturing a set of bathroom tiles inlaid with rhinestones, she was delighted with the little bamboo and bone tablets, and dice. The case was leather and very dainty. She could not imagine gangling Tom handling it but he could hardly fail to be pleasèd, it looked so nice, and it slid conveniently into her shopping-bag so he would not see it if they met when she got home.

Then she went to find a bus and to ring the Dog

and Rocket in case anyone was worried by her long absence. It was Dad who answered the telephone.

'Hallo?'

'Dad, what are you up to?'

'Don't shout, Lil. It rang just as I was passing.'

'Whaddya mean, passing? How can you pass the top of the stairs?'

'Well, I've just been walking up and down a bit, practising. No pain at all – ouch!'

'No pain, huh?'

'Just a twinge as I sat down. Don't fuss. Tom's keeping an eye on me. I'll have to be down by Saturday, won't I?'

'It won't matter by Saturday. Look, Dad . . .'

'Well, I want to be. Stop nagging. Did you get him something nice?'

'Don't let on, will you? A mah-jong set.'

'What the hell's that?' Dad said, but she could not tell him because just then the money ran out.

Dad spent Friday finding his feet along the landing. In the evening he dressed and came carefully downstairs, appearing behind the bar just as David and Moira Fellows arrived in the Saloon. David became Dr Fellows again at once.

'What do you think you're doing?'

Dad cringed. 'Come off it, David. June's home tomorrow. With a bit of luck she'll never know.'

'Don't be ridiculous,' David said. 'She'll have to know. You've got to take things carefully from now on and you can't go on working these two into the ground.'

'It was good for them,' Dad said. 'Especially Tom. Baptism of fire.' He nodded towards Tom who was serving in the Public. 'It's done our Lil good, too.'

'How?' Lilian said, depositing a tray of empty glasses on the bar.

'Softened you up a bit,' Dad said, 'and hardened him.'

'You ought to be in bed,' David Fellows said, 'but now you're here we'll have a Scotch on the rocks and a glass of red wine.'

'What's going to happen tomorrow?' Lilian asked Dad, later on. In spite of meaning frowns from David Fellows, Dad was still behind the bar at nine-thirty and looked good for closing time. 'You may be back on your feet but you won't be able to drive.'

'Your mum'll be in on the six-forty,' he said. 'Tom can drive in to meet her.'

'She doesn't know what he looks like,' Lilian said, 'and he doesn't know her.'

'Well, ring her before she leaves and tell her to look out for a tall lad with a long nose, a black eye and a fat lip. She ought to be able to spot him.'

'Oh, Dad, she'll have a fit.'

'Could it be,' Dad said, 'that you want to go too?'

'I didn't mean that.'

'You go ahead,' Dad said. 'Len and I can manage here.'

'No you can't,' David said from the end of the bar.

'I'll have two Scotch eggs and then you can get back to bed; right?'

'Wrong. Get the man his eggs, Lil.'

Tom came through from the Public and David saw him full-face for the first time. 'Good god, what have you been doing to yourself? What's going on, Bob? This used to be a respectable house. June won't trust you on your own again.'

Lilian, closing the glass case and arranging the eggs on napkins, thought, She'll be back, this time tomorrow. This time tomorrow, James and Emma will be back, too.

The mah-jong set, gift-wrapped, was at the back of her wardrobe. It had taken so long to locate that she had forgotten to buy a card so after breakfast she went across to Ambrose, but his stocks were running low. They were all addressed to Dear Dad, the Best Mum in the World, the Greatest Gran ever and My Sweetheart. In the end she bought three: *Happy Birthday Eight-Year-Old*, *Now You are Four!* and *Ten Today Hooray Hooray!* She took them back, shoved them all in the largest envelope, wrote *Add them* up and left it with the post on the kitchen-table where he would find it when he had crated the empties. She wanted to wait until they had a quiet moment before giving him the mah-jong set, so that she could watch him unwrap it.

She went into the Saloon where Mrs Allott, who had come in on a Saturday as a special favour because

Mum was due home, was hoovering, and began to wipe down the shelves. Dad was upstairs with strict instructions to remain there until they had finished bottling up, in case he was tempted to try and lift something.

When she came back to the kitchen for the glass cloths she met Tom on the way out with his mail.

'Happy birthday,' she said.

'It was nice of you to remember,' Tom said. 'I like your cards. That must have taken some thought.'

She nodded, although the addition sum had been a spur-of-the-moment decision born of desperation. 'Did you get anything interesting?'

'My mum said she'll give me my present when I get home — bribery, see. My brother sent a record token.'

'That was nice.'

'Not so very. It's the one I sent him on *his* birthday with the names changed round. My sister forgot, which is only fair. I forgot hers.'

'Do you want to put your cards up in the sitting-room?' Lilian asked. She did not say 'Anything from Andrea?' and he did not mention it. She was glad that she had sent three cards; without them he'd have had only his mum's and the second-hand record token. She wanted to run up and fetch the mah-jong set but there was no time. The Public had not been swept, there were the beds to be changed and Tom ought by now to be bottling up. They parted breathlessly.

By six o'clock, when it was time to go to the station, she still had not found a moment to give it to him, but it had come downstairs although it was still lying on the kitchen-table, unnoticed. Tom had put the telephone back in the sitting-room and replaced all the staples that anchored the cable. While he and Lilian were manhandling the freezer back into place over the uneven tiles, the Yak had come out to investigate, with his usual lack of discretion, and the freezer had come down on Tom's fingers. He had spent the rest of the afternoon with his hand in cold water, trying to reduce the swelling so that he could drive to Ashford that evening. He came downstairs now, heavily bandaged. Lilian, regarding him, felt that he had not had much of a birthday. There had been no word from Andrea.

The train was on time. Tom had bought platform tickets and they stood at the foot of the steps on the down platform, watching the passengers. Mum, of course, was one of the last, at the far end of the train. There was no sign of James and Emma.

'Perhaps she pushed them out somewhere,' Tom suggested as they went forward to help with the luggage. Lilian kissed her mother and looked round.

'Where are the kids?'

'Oh, I don't know.' Mum looked worn out and close to tears. What sort of a holiday had it been for her? Lilian wondered. 'They were off the train almost before it stopped and now they're hiding. They must be on the platform somewhere. They couldn't have passed you on the way out, could they?'

'Wait till everyone's gone and then we'll find them.' Lilian ground her teeth. She could guess what the journey from Edinburgh had been like. Then she remembered Tom, hovering in the background. 'Oh, Mum, this is Tom Collins — our bar help. He drove me to meet you.'

'Where's your Dad?' She looked alarmed.

'In the bar, I hope,' Lilian said, impatiently. 'Come here, Tom.'

'Pleased to meet you,' Mum said, still glancing worriedly all round. Tom held out his hand. Mum started to shake it, noticed the bandage, then his lip, then his eye. Her worried look turned to one of alarm. 'What have you been *doing*?'

'Oh, it didn't happen all at once,' Tom said quickly. 'Just one damn thing after another. I'm accident-prone — known for it.'

'It's all right, he doesn't smash things,' Lilian said. 'Just himself. Where are the little monsters?'

'Could that be them?' Tom nodded down the platform to where James and Emma were playing stock cars with a luggage trolley.

'Oh . . .' Mum cried, as it slewed towards the edge of the platform. Tom reached them in half a dozen strides.

'Well,' he said, 'that's good of you. Just what we need.' He hauled them off the trolley, wheeled it back and began to stack the cases on it.

'We'll never get it up the steps,' Lilian said.

'Of course not. Just taking the wind out of their sails,' Tom muttered. 'Making them feel useful. I don't think they want to feel useful, do you?'

'Who's that freak?' James said. Emma simply stared at him and giggled.

He'll leave, Lilian thought. He'll give in his notice after a couple of days of this. She had forgotten that he was a teacher and used to worse than James and Emma. He stared back at them and his face became expressionless.

'Stop that stupid noise,' he said. 'James, don't speak to me like that.'

'I speak how I like,' James said, with some truth.

'Not to me,' said Tom. 'Remember that, will you?' They had reached the foot of the steps. He picked up the two suitcases. 'Right,' he said, 'can you manage the small one, Lil? James, Emma, you can bring that big hold-all between you.'

'I'm not carrying anything,' Emma said.

'She's too little,' protested Mum, who had also had the wind taken out of her sails.

'I'm too little,' Emma said, promptly.

'Pick it up,' Tom snapped. He was not smiling. 'How did you manage crossing London, Mrs Goodwin?'

'Oh, someone helped me . . .' Mum said, vaguely. She looked at Tom. Tom was still looking at James and Emma.

'I said pick it up. We're not going anywhere until you do. Lilian and your mum can take the car. We'll stop here.'

Lilian could hardly believe what she was seeing. James and Emma took a handle each and lifted the bag. 'Thank you,' Tom said calmly, and allowed them a small cold smile. In silence they all began to mount the steps.

At the car the children immediately began to quarrel about who should sit in front.

'Neither of you is sitting in front,' Tom said. 'It's not safe. Get in the back at once – *at once*, I said.' He turned to Lilian. 'D'you mind going in the back with them – let your mum sit in the front?'

'Anything you say,' Lilian said, minding very much. There was a few minutes' silence as they left the car-park and then James reared up and leaned over the back of the front seat between Mum and Tom.

'There was this fat old geezer on the train,' he began.

'Sit down,' Tom said.

'Don't you tell me what to do,' James said. Emma joined in and they began to chant: 'Don't-tell-us-what-to-dooooo.' Tom stopped the car in Elwick Road.

'Sit down and be quiet,' he said. They took no notice. He climbed out, walked round to the near side and opened the rear door. 'Out,' he said.

James and Emma shut up but they did not move. Tom reached into the car and dragged them out. Then he slammed the door. 'Lock it, Lil. I told you,' he said evenly, to James and Emma. He walked back to the driver's door, got in and started the engine again. Lilian saw her unpleasant brother and sister instantly

117

transformed into two startled and frightened children. Emma's mouth opened in a howl of fear.

'Excuse me,' Tom said to Mum. He leaned across her and wound down the window. 'Either you do as I say or you walk home. Is that understood? Right. Get in, then.' Lilian unlocked the door. James and Emma slid in beside her and cowered. Not another word was uttered, all the way home.

They had recovered themselves by the time they disembarked, however, and conveniently forgetting the rule about not going into the bars raced down the passage shouting, 'Dad! Dad! We're back!'

Dad hurried, as best he could, from the Saloon, to herd them back into the passage. Tom, who had carried the luggage upstairs, slipped past them and took Dad's place behind the bar. Lilian, going to give Len a much-needed hand in the Public, heard Mum in the kitchen. 'Oh, Bob, what on earth's going on here? Why's the dog shut in the sitting-room? Who's that overbearing lout that Lilian's giving the eye to?'

Dad closed the kitchen door and she heard nothing more, but her face felt dry and hot. Giving Tom the eye? Was that what she was doing? When he came through the archway to fetch more ice, she was busy changing a keg and would not look at him. It was nearly nine before they met face to face, when there was a slight lull in the traffic and Dad sent them both to get some supper before things warmed up again. They were slightly taken aback by this; it was the first time for a fortnight that they had had time for any supper.

Mum was upstairs unpacking, but James and Emma were at the table. Emma was messing about with the remains of a plate of shepherd's pie.

'Who cooked this muck?'

'I did,' Tom said. 'If you don't want it don't eat it, but stop throwing it about.'

'It looks like what the cat left.'

'Any more complaints,' said Tom, 'and I'll poke it up your nose with a sharp stick.'

James, surprisingly, said nothing. Then Lilian noticed that he was busy with something on his lap. At the same moment a torn sheet of red wrapping paper fell to the floor and he held up a brown leather case by the handle.

'What's this, then?'

It was the mah-jong set. Lilian made a grab for it but he jerked it away. 'Is it for us?' James said. 'Where'd you get it? What is it?'

'Give it to me,' Lilian said. 'Give it to me at once, James. You had no right to touch it. It was wrapped up. You must have known it wasn't for you.'

'It might have been.' James was fiddling with the clasps.

Emma slung her plate to one side and snatched at the case. 'Let me see.'

Tom, serving shepherd's pie at the stove, turned round just in time to see the clasps give way. The case opened like a mouth and crashing down on to the table came tiles, spills and dice.

Then there was silence, except for the clack of falling pieces skidding off the table. Lilian, enraged and exhausted, began to cry. Tom, ignoring the children, put down the serving spoon, came over and put his arm round her.

'Lil, don't; don't love. Nothing's broken, I think.'

Lilian could not stop. 'It was your birthday present.'

'Mine?' He stared at his present scattered to all corners of the kitchen. 'For me? From you? It's lovely.' He looked again. 'What is it?'

Lilian wiped her face on *his* sleeve. 'Don't you know?'

He picked up a tile. 'Isn't it beautiful? I've never seen anything like it.'

'But can't you play? It's a mah-jong set.'

'Mah-jong?' She saw very well that he could not play. 'For me?'

'But you told Mac that time . . . when he asked you to play darts . . .'

'Oh god.' Tom looked conscience-stricken. 'I was joking. I can't play – and I was pretty sure he couldn't. I didn't want to get caught playing *anything*. I'm not even any good at draughts.'

Lilian thought she would cry again, but he looked so appalled that she began to laugh instead. 'It's all right. It doesn't matter. You can keep it to look at.'

'No, no. I'll learn. I *will*. We'll both learn. Look,

there's an instruction leaflet.' It had coasted under the table. 'We'll be East Kent Champions before I leave.'

Lilian was still convinced that he would probably be leaving within forty-eight hours. 'I should think we'd be the only *players* in East Kent.' She knelt to pick up the pieces.

'Don't do that!' Tom said, angrily. James and Emma were sidling towards the garden door but he intercepted them. 'Those two can do it.'

'Not likely,' James said. 'It wasn't my fault. It's got duff catches.'

Tom caught him by the shoulder, quite gently but very firmly. He took Emma by the hand and leaned over them looking enormous and not to be trifled with.

'Now, see here,' he said, 'you are going to pick up every single piece and you are going to fit them all back into the case, in all the right places – every piece where it belongs, and then you are going to bed.'

'You can't send us to bed,' Emma said, but she did not sound too sure.

'I didn't say send,' Tom said. 'If you don't go when I tell you I shall put you there myself. And if either of you ever touches anything belonging to me again you will be –' his voice became quite soft '– ever so sorry. Understand?'

'I'll tell Mum,' James began.

'I don't care if you take a full-page ad in the *Kentish Express*,' said Tom.

'I want Mum to put us to bed,' Emma said, but she

only *said* it. 'She always does. Lil, don't let him. I want Mum, Lil.' Lilian smiled at her serenely.

'She's too tired and you're old enough to put yourselves to bed,' Tom said.

'She reads to us.' Even James's chin was trembling.

'No one is going to read to you tonight,' Tom said, 'but if you behave yourselves, *I* may read to you tomorrow night. You'd better look out some interesting books – I'm not reading codswallop. Now, get going on this lot.'

They settled down on the floor. Tom and Lilian stayed out of the way and ate standing up at the stove. They were just putting the plates to soak when Len looked in from the bar.

'Can one of you come out? Bob's gone up to have a word with June and we're filling up again.' They both went through, Tom to the Public, Lilian to the Saloon, just in time to serve Major and Mrs Heathcote.

'I've got your *Cupressus* in the car,' said the Major. 'I'll fetch them in presently.'

'Don't let Dad see,' Lilian warned him. 'I haven't mentioned them yet.'

'A surprise?'

'Sort of.'

When she next looked across into the Public the rush was dealt with. In the warm smoky light Tom, with a pint, was chatting to Grievous, Len was serving Mac and May and Dad would be down at any moment. Tomorrow Mum would be in as well and things would be back to normal . . . and then she thought, no: not quite normal. Tom'll still be here and look what he's done to James and Emma already. It might still be a good summer. She thought of Shaun, absent friend, and absent friends made her think of Andrea, but Shaun was in France and Andrea was in Rotherham . . .

She was roused by a man approaching from the French windows.

'You take coaches?' he asked hopefully.

She nodded. 'How many are you?'

'Forty-five. It's the Lenham Chart Cricket Club and supporters.'

'Bring them in then,' she said. Tom looked through the archway.

'Hey up!'

'Hey up.'

'All quiet on the Western Front?'

'Not for much longer,' Lilian said. 'We've got a coach full of cricketers coming in, right now. Can you face that?'

'What happens if I say no?'

'I'll fire you.'

He grinned. 'I can face it.'

She grinned back. 'That's OK then. Set 'em up, Tom.'

THE TIGER IN THE WELL
Philip Pullman

Sued for divorce when she's never been married, by a man she's never heard of, Sally Lockhart's life is completely uprooted. There seems nothing she can do to prevent the loss of her money, her home, her financial consultancy business, and, most desperately, her dear two-year-old daughter, Harriet.

Sally is a surprising and wonderfully modern heroine, and her fight against unknown and relentless evil in Victorian London makes an exhilarating and unforgettable novel.

MY NAME IS NOT ANGELICA
Scott O'Dell

Raisha was to be married to the proud young chief Konje before they were captured by slave-traders. But on the Caribbean island plantation, Konje soon joins a band of runaways. As the slave revolt grows, so does the harshness of the owners' response, and by the time Raisha is reunited with her lover, the slaves have only one desperate option to take to remain free.

STAR FOR A MONTH
Ben Taylor

When schoolgirl Sarah Scott joins the cast of TV soap *Eldon House* to take up her first prize in *Teen Scene* magazine's competition, her biggest worry is learning her lines.

But she soon gets caught up in the glamorous but harsh world of the superstar, hounded by the tabloid photographers who snap her in her most private moments, and reporters who record her every word and use them out of context. Soon her face rivals only that of the Princess of Wales on the front pages, and she realizes that her life is no longer her own – she has to share it with 120 million TV viewers!

DAZ 4 ZOE
Robert Swindells

'Here is a teenage novel with everything: love, loyalty, nail-biting suspense, some excellent writing, and a huge moral poser about where our Two Nations society will end. Set in a not-so-distant future world, the story is told through the alternate voices of the two young lovers. How the two teen-agers meet and keep contact across the divide is nail-biting enough, but the story of their escape from the ties of their own communities and the security forces is brilliant, pulling few punches about the cost to others which their freedom must exact' — Aisling Foster, *Independent*

TAKING THE FERRY HOME
Pam Conrad

Ali is instantly wildly jealous of Simone's beauty, wealth and confidence. But Simone is determined that the two should be friends for the summer. And so they become, for a seemingly perfect holiday of fun, friendship and romance. Simone even promises to help Ali get the gorgeous Brendan. But promises are hard for Simone.

In a dramatic climax to this gripping novel, Ali begins to realize that Simone's life isn't to be envied after all.

MADAME DOUBTFIRE
Anne Fine

Lydia, Christopher and Natalie Hilliard are used to domestic turmoil and have been torn between their warring parents ever since the divorce. But all that changes when their mother takes on a most unusual cleaning lady. Despite her extraordinary appearance, Madame Doubtfire turns out to be a talented and efficient housekeeper and, for a short time at least, the arrangement is a resounding success. But as the Hilliard children soon discover, there's more to Madame Doubtfire than domestic talents . . .

ROUND BEHIND THE ICE-HOUSE
Anne Fine

Tom wants to forget – to get back into the past when he and Cass were still so close. What are the secrets she is keeping from him? Tom has to face the fact that as he and Cass grow up, they have to grow apart. He may be her twin brother but he doesn't own her and he never can. A powerful and unusual story about the tensions of changing relationships.

MEL
Liz Berry

Seventeen-year-old Melody is desperate for her life to change, but she isn't prepared for the turmoil into which she is thrown following her mother's nervous breakdown. Left alone in their squalid house, Mel determines to repair and redecorate. Then, while searching for furniture in a local junk shop, she meets the dangerously attractive Mitch Hamilton, lead guitarist with top rock group, Assassination. Mitch is keen to help with the house, but Mel is suspicious of his enthusiasm. So when Mitch announces his intention to marry Mel, no one is more astounded than Mel herself. Except Mitch's jealous ex-girlfriend.

A PACK OF LIES
Geraldine McCaughrean

Ailsa doesn't usually pick up men in public libraries – but then MCC Berkshire is rather out of the ordinary and has a certain irresistible charm. Once inside Ailsa and her mother's antiques shop, he also reveals an amazing talent for holding customers spellbound with his extravagant stories – and selling antiques into the bargain!